THATS MY TYPE 2

A HOOD LOVE STORY

JAMMIE JAYE

Cole Hart
SIGNATURE NOVELS

Thats My Type 2

Copyright © 2019 by Jammie Jaye

All rights reserved.

Published in the United States of America.

Published by Cole Hart Signature, LLC.

Mailing List

To stay up to date on new releases, plus get information on contests, sneak peeks, and more,

Go To The Website Below...

WWW.COLEHARTSIGNATURE.COM

❀ Created with Vellum

PEACHES

"*J* heard them talking about a party. We should go with them," I recommended. I didn't club much, but for some reason, I wanted to dance and let my hair down.

"We can… shit, you know I'm always down to show out," Nellie replied as we sat down to get our nails done. We had just gotten up from getting pedicures. Today was our free day without our loves. Although we both knew that they would be calling soon. I could honestly say that I was in love. Cream was everything that I could want in a man. I think what made me love him the most was that he never asked for sex.

"Girl…" I mumbled when I looked up to see Cream's ex walk in the door. I knew then that shit was going to get nasty as soon as she laid eyes on me. Nellie looked up and started laughing. Her ass was crazy. I loved it though; she was a loose cannon. If she thought it, she said it, but the crazy thing was, when you looked at her, you would never know.

"That bitch better stay in her lane." I just shook my head.

"Don't I know you from somewhere?" Nique asked as she

walked up to us. I looked at Nellie and Nellie looked at me, and we burst out laughing. She just *had* to say something to us.

"Nah you don't know me," Nellie stated without looking her way. Nique walked off and went to the pedicure chair where her friend was. That's when they started the petty, childish shit. I hate grown bullies. Like bitch, you too damn grown for that.

"Girl, that's who Cream chose? I just knew the nigga had better taste than that," one of the girls said.

"Then to think she's really doing something. The bitch got my leftovers," Nique said. It took everything for me to not say shit. I knew that was what she wanted. I wasn't going to let her get under my skin. They both just kept talking. I was happy that we were almost done. Just as the nail tech was finishing, my phone rung. It was a FACETIME from Cream. I answered and sat the phone up so that I could see him and she could as well.

"Damn, you not done yet?" he asked as the call connected.

"I'm almost done baby," I assured him.

"Good, cause I miss you. And tell Nell that my brother said hurry the fuck up," he joked. Nell looked at the nail tech and told her to hurry up. Her and Puff were so damn cute.

"Aite baby, I'll be waiting for you," he said before we ended the call. I looked over, and Nique looked like she was ready to cry. We finished up, paid, and then proceeded to walk out.

"I will have the last laugh," Nique said as I walked past her. I just kept walking. Her threats didn't faze me.

As I made it to my car, I could tell that something was wrong. I walked around the car to see that my tire were all flat. It had Nique's name written all over it. She was *really* trying me. I pulled my phone out of my purse and called Cream.

"Damn, you miss daddy already?"

"Umm... yo crazy ass ex slashed my tires," I told him. Just as I did, she walked out of the nail shop. They all looked at us and busted out laughing. I just nodded because I knew that sooner or later, she would have to see me.

"I'm pulling up," he told me as he hung up. I leaned against my car and started scrolling through Instagram. I looked up to see Cream coming down the street, so I moved to the driver's side so that I could get my purse out the car. Before I could open the car door, I heard Nell yell out. When I looked up, it was too late. I just closed my eyes and waited for the impact of the car to hit me. I just knew that I was dead. The car had barely missed me. I opened my eyes as Cream was jumping out of the car. He ran to me and hugged me so tight. I couldn't do shit but cry.

"Baby, are you ok?" he asked as he looked over my body. My heart felt like it was beating outside my body. Cream picked me up and walked me to his car. Once I was inside, the other back door opened, and Cream climbed in. Puff got in the driver's seat, and Nellie got in on the passenger's side. I just laid my head back so that I could catch my breath. The whole ride, no one talked. Cream held me close to him as we rode. "I will never let anyone hurt you," he whispered to me as I drifted off to sleep.

"Wake up, baby." I opened my eyes and they damn near popped out my head. We were at one of the biggest houses that I had ever seen in my life. It was like one of the houses that I saw on *Love and Hip Hop* or some shit. He got out and walked around to help me out the car. As we walked up to the door, I observed the beautiful landscaping.

"Whose house is this?" I asked as we walked up to the door.

"Mine."

I looked back at Nellie, and she just shrugged. Hell, I

thought his ass lived at the hotel as much as he was there. I walked in behind him and was floored. His house was beautiful. The whole back wall was floor to ceiling windows. His house overlooked a large lake. He cut on the TV and walked to the kitchen. I plopped down on the couch and closed my eyes. Just as I did, I got a notification on my phone. It was on Facebook. When I opened it, I couldn't believe my eyes. I had been getting these messages for a while. But this was the *first* time that someone had tried to kill my ass.

Facebook User: Next time I won't miss you bitch

Cream sat next to me, and I handed him my phone. He read it and then sat it on the table. He was doing everything to get my mind off the fact that I damn near died, but it was all that I could think about. Who in the hell wanted to kill me? I didn't have any enemies as far as I knew, so why the hell was this happening to me?

"You wanna go for a swim?" Cream asked me, pulling me from my thoughts. I just shook my head. I wasn't being mean; I just wasn't in the mood for all that. He nodded and pulled me closer to him. I felt relaxed and safe.

"I'm going to the house so that I can get us some clothes. Bitch, we still going out... we not finna let whoever that was ruin our day," Nell said as she and Puff walked out the door. I just shook my head. I knew that no matter how much I fussed that she was still going to make me go out.

"Aw... so you going out with daddy tonight?" he joked. I couldn't do shit but smile.

"Naw, I'm going to meet me a baller," I joked back. He just looked at me. I knew that he was going to start talking shit by the look on his face.

"You gone get a nigga murked," he said before getting up. He walked up the stairs, and I strolled to the kitchen to get me something to drink. I didn't want to be all through his shit, but I was thirsty. I found a bottle of wine and popped it open. I poured me a glass and took a seat at the island. I looked around and admired how nice his kitchen was. I would die for a place like this.

"So you just made yo' self at home?" he said as he walked in the kitchen.

"I mean, why not? You did just say that you would kill someone over me, so I took that as an open invitation to make myself at home," I said, sipping on my wine.

"You are correct baby." He walked over then sat down next to me at the island.

We sat there and talked until Puff and Nellie got back. Since it was still early, I decided to take a nap.

CREAM

*S*ince Peaches was sleep, I decided to go to my office and get some work done. I needed to find a few contractors for our club. I wanted to do some upgrades. I had a few that I used before, but I wanted to find someone else because I had them all on other shit. I jotted down a few then pulled up the cameras at the trap so that I could see what was going on. I liked to keep watch on my shit. Niggas always did shit when they thought that no one was watching.

"Yo, I'm finna head home so that I can change and Nell can shower," my brother walked in my office and told me.

"Sounds good." I was watching the nigga that was working in the trap count. I wanted to make sure that he wasn't on no funny shit. Puff made his way around my desk so that he could see what had my attention. Once the nigga was done, Puff walked out of my office, and I closed my computer down.

I locked the door behind him and woke Peaches up. She was stretched out on my couch, sleeping peacefully. I hated to wake her, but I needed to know if we planned to go anywhere. I kissed her on her lips and her eyes popped open.

When she realized that it was me, she pulled me down on the couch with her. She looked me in my eyes before kissing me with so much passion that my dick was rock hard, just that fast. I rubbed my hands down her body, causing a chill to go through her body. My hands made their way to her center. I unbuttoned her jeans and slipped my finger in between her folds. She was so fucking wet. I pulled her pants down so that I could get full access. I had been waiting on this moment for a while. I helped her take her shirt off. I stood back for a second because I wanted to see her naked. This was something that I would never forget. I took my shirt off and made my way back to her.

"I want you," she moaned out as I kissed on her neck. The sound of her voice was doing something to me. I kissed all over her body as I battled with myself on if I wanted to feel her or taste her. She didn't give me a chance to choose because she pulled me down, causing my dick to slide straight in. I had to chill for a second because her shit was so warm and wet that a nigga was ready to let loose. Once I gained my composure, I went in. I wanted to make sure that I was the *only* nigga that she wanted. She was moaning my name so fucking loud that I was sure that the neighbors damn near a mile away could hear her. It was like music to my ears, and I didn't want it to end.

"Ummm… it feels so good," she said, pulling me in deeper. She started grinding, and that was it. I released my seeds in her.

"Fuck!" I blurted. "In the morning, we packing yo shit up and you moving here," I said as I pulled my dick out of her. She didn't have to like it, but it was going to happen. I needed to be able to slide in her whenever I wanted.

"Cream, I can't do that. I have to be there to help Nell with the bills," she explained.

"You can, and you will. I will take care of your part of the bills," I assured her. She just looked at me. I waited to see if she was going to say something else, but she didn't; she just got up and walked upstairs. I followed behind her. She opened each door until she found the one that she was looking for. Once we were in my room, she walked in the bathroom. I was just happy that she didn't keep trying to debate me about the subject. I heard the shower come on, so I decided to go and find something to wear.

"Can you go and get my clothes from downstairs?" she asked as she walked out of the bathroom. I went downstairs and did as she requested. When I returned upstairs and back to the room, she was laying in the bed with her legs wide open. My dick rocked back up as I made my way to her. It was so juicy. I just wanted to kiss all over it. I dove straight in. Yeah, a nigga was in love. Nique's shit was cool, but bae's shit was *life*. I ate her pussy until she screamed for me to stop. When she tapped out, I headed to shower because we need to leave in the next hour. I showered and got dressed while she did her makeup. An hour and a half later, we were done and heading out the door. Since this was our first night out, I decided to let her pick.

"Baby, what you wanna ride in?" I asked. She smiled and pointed to my Lambo. It had been a while since I drove it, so I was down. I grabbed the keys, and we got in. I called my brother to see where he was as we jumped on the express-way. It took us no time to get there. My brother and Nellie arrived at the same time as Peaches and me. We both got out first then helped our women out. Every female had envy in their eyes as we made our way to the door. I knew that we were going to be the talk of the town. These nosey mother-fuckas always worried about other people's business. I escorted Peaches to the VIP section so that I could make my rounds to make sure everything was good.

"Where you going, baby?" she asked as I was walking off.

"I need to make sure everything is good," I advised her.

"I can go with you. I want to see your office anyway," she said, walking to where I was standing. I smiled because I knew that she was trying to fuck. We made our way around the room as I checked to make sure that everything was going smooth and that the VIP's were getting taken care of. Once I was done, we headed to my office. Soon as the door closed, she was all over me. She dropped to her knees and unbuckled my pants. Once she had my dick out, she wrapped her mouth around it. Her lips were so fucking soft. "Shit baby... just like that," I moaned. She was making slurping sounds that were driving me crazy. Her head game was just as good as her pussy. Once we were done, she cleaned up, and we headed to join the party.

There were people everywhere. We walked in VIP to see Puff all over Nellie. I was shocked because Puff didn't do the whole PDA thing. He didn't want to be seen with no female in public. She was good for him, and it was obvious that it was love.

"Gone sit down, I'll get you a drink baby," I told Peaches. She kissed me then walked over to where Nellie was. I was standing near the balcony, looking at the dance floor. I saw Nique walking up, so I motioned for security to stop her. I was not about to deal with her shit tonight. I watched as he dragged her off. I fixed Peaches a drink and went to sit next to her. Soon as I sat down, her phone beeped. She opened the message and locked her phone back.

"You good baby?" I asked. She just nodded before she started drinking her drink; after a few drinks, her and Nellie got up to dance. I couldn't help but admire her. She was so beautiful. My baby was so full. I couldn't do shit but laugh; she was living her best life. The whole night, they had the time of their life. When the night was over, Peaches couldn't even walk. I took her to the office so that she could lay down while we made sure that the club was cleared. Puff had done the same. Once we were good, we grabbed them and headed out.

PUFF

$\mathcal{I}$ was headed home but couldn't help but notice the car that had been following me. I pulled out my phone and called my brother.

"Yo, I think a nigga following me," I told him as I hit a corner, hoping to lose the car. Nellie was knocked out, which I was happy about because I knew that she would have been freaking out.

"Where you at?"

I told him where I was before I ended the call. I was doing my best to get away, but the nigga was keeping up. My phone rung, waking Nellie up. I answered just as she sat up and looked around.

"Baby, what going on?" Before I could answer her, the car slammed into the back of my car. I did my best to maintain control, but I couldn't. We swerved to the left and then my car started to flip. As the sound of metal crumbling and ripping surrounded me, the only thing on my mind was my baby. I needed her to be okay. After what felt like forever, the car stopped rolling. I looked over, and Nellie was bleeding from her head.

"Baby?" I called. She didn't answer.

I did my best to move, but it was hard; part of the dash was pushing down on my legs. "Nellie!" I called. She didn't move. I flinched from the pain as I squeeze then pulled myself up until my legs were free. I forced the dented driver's side door open before fallen out of the car. "Fuck!" I blurted from the pain. I gathered all the strength that I could and then pulled myself up onto my feet. I had to help my baby.

"I been waiting a long time to do this." A familiar voice came from behind me. I turned as fast as I could, but soon as I did, I felt bullets piercing through my body. I felled to the ground, and my eyes landed on Nellie. *I love you, baby.* I fought as hard as I could to keep my eyes open, but I failed. Everything went black.

1 CREAM

I was doing my best not to panic. I didn't want to scare Peaches. I headed in the direction of my brother's house. When his phone hung up, I heard Nellie scream. I was happy that I didn't have it on speaker because she would be panicking right now and that was not what I needed. I dialed his number back to see if he would answer, but I wasn't that lucky. I drove down as many streets as I could so that I could find them. The fact that it pitch black didn't help at all. That was one of the things I hated about this area... there was no street lights. When I made it near where he said that he was, I saw his car flipped over. I jumped out of the car and ran straight to him. I could see Nellie out the side of my eye, but I needed to make sure that he was good first.

"Call 911!" I yelled to Peaches as she made her way out the car. She already had the phone to her ear as I said that. I could see her making her way over to Nellie. From what I could see, she was bleeding from her head. I prayed that she was not dead because if she was, my brother was going to fucking flip. I wasn't going to even put in my mind that he was dead. I knew that he was a fighter and that he was going to make it.

"They on the way baby. Come on Nell baby, you gotta keep yo eyes open." I heard Peaches coaching behind me. There was so many thing going through my head that I did know what the hell to think. Who in their right mind would do some shit like this? I knew that it had to be someone who didn't know how we got down.

Two ambulances pulled up at the same time. One team went to see about Nellie and the other came to check on my brother. "We have to get him to the hospital fast... Will, he still have a pulse," I heard one EMT say. I was happy as hell to hear that; at least I knew that he was still alive. Once they had him, I went over to where Nellie was. There was blood all over her face. Peaches was just standing to the side look-ing. I knew that she was scared. I grabbed her hand and guided her to the car. I wanted to make sure that I made it to the hospital soon as they did. Once we were in the car, I called my grandfather and Scale. I wanted to call my mother, but I decided to wait until I knew what was going on.

"Baby, do you think they will be ok?" Peaches asked as soon as we pulled up to the hospital.

"They are going to be ok baby, don't worry," I told her as we got out the car. We rushed in so that we could see them go to the back. Once I let the nurse know that we were there, she let us know that they took him to surgery. This was the first time something like this had happened. My brother had been shot before but not life threatening. Someone had liter-ally tried to kill my brother, and I wasn't going to stop until I found out who. We sat there for about ten minute before people start coming in. I knew that Scale was going to alert the crew.

My grandfather walked in the door and I could see the worry on his face. He signaled for me to come to where he was. I knew that he wanted to know what happened. The only problem with that was, I didn't know. "What happened son?" he asked just as I knew that he would.

"I don't know Pops. He called and said that someone was following them. Then I heard her screaming and the phone hung up. I rode around till I found them," I explained. He just nodded and pulled out his phone. I went to sit back down because I was starting to get light headed. My phone rang and looked down to see that it was Nique calling. I just hit ignore because I didn't have time for her shit today.

"I want to call her mama, but I don't know if he will follow them here. I don't want her ex to find her. She said that he would kill her," Peaches told me. My brother couldn't have known that; if he did, he would have told me. Just as I was about to reply, the doctors walked out.

"Family of Amber Turner," a doctor came out and said. Peaches got up and I just looked because I didn't know what was going on. I though her damn name was *Nellie*. I knew that Puff had gotten a check done on her, but he never said anything so I assumed that everything was good.

"Right here," she said, confirming that they were talking about Nellie, so I got up and joined her.

"Ms. Turner is doing ok. She has a concussion, all the blood made it look way worst than it was. She has been placed in a room. I can take y'all back now," he advised. I could see the relief in Peaches' face. Scale went back with us and Pops stay just in case they came out with an update on Puff. When we walked in the room, she was just looking up at the ceiling.

"Nell, I'm so happy that you are ok." Peaches cried soon as she made it over to the bed. She hugged her so tight that you could see that it was hurting Nellie, but she didn't say anything; she just let the tears flow.

"Please tell me that he is ok," Nellie said soon as Peaches let her go.

"We haven't heard anything yet. He is still in surgery the last that we heard. What the hell happened?" I asked. I looked back and Scale was closing the sliding door. I guess he knew that I was going to say that. I knew that soon the police were going to be coming around. I needed to know what happened, so I would know what to tell her to say. I didn't need them finding who did this before I did. This was *personal.*

"The last thing I remember is laying down in the office. Next thing I know, a ringing phone is waking me up. I look over to Puff and he has this worried look on his face, so I asked him what was wrong. Before we know it, the car is hit hard from the back, and we start flipping over and over and that is all that I remember," she explained with so much sorrow in her voice. I could tell that she was scared.

"Ok... when the police come because they are going to come for sure, tell them that you don't remember anything but the car hitting y'all then you blacked out."

We all talked for a while before me and Scale went back to the waiting area to see if the doctor had came back out with an update on my brother. When I walked out, there was so many people. I looked around until I found Dee and Scut.

"Aye, I need y'all to go back there and keep watch on my girl and her friend. Shoot first ask questions later," I stated. I told them the room number then dapped them up before they walked off. Once they were gone, I took a seat next to my grandpops. For some reason, my attention kept falling on Raye. It was something about that nigga that I didn't like. The only reason he wasn't dead was because he was Scale's nigga.

"I'm starting to test that nigga. He been on some sneaky

shit lately," Scale said, taking a seat next to me. That shit caught mine and my grandfather's attention.

"What you mean by that?" Pops asked.

"He just been moving funny. Like the other day, I saw him somewhere, but he had just said the he was somewhere else. I didn't ask for that lie... he volunteered it. I didn't even ask the nigga where he was. Then some money came up short, the nigga didn't tell me about until I asked him about it," Scale explained. I just nodded because I was going to see what was up with his ass. I signaled for one of my workers to come over and instructed him to keep a close eye on Raye. I knew sooner or later that his ass was gone have to die.

"Family of Donald Latham," the doctor called out, pulling us from the conversation that we were having.

"We are his family," Pops assured him. He ushered us into a room and all I could think was the worst. I was kind of happy that he did that so that everyone would know what was going on. The only people that were in the room was me, Pops, Pops' girlfriend Ms. Rose Scale, and my Uncle Edward.

"He was hit five times... one of the bullets ripped through his lungs. We repaired that, but there was so much damage to his body that we put him in a medically inducted coma. After a week or so, we will pull him out of the coma. That will give him time to heal a little," he explained. I just drooped my head. It wasn't because I was sad; it was because I doubted my brother. I knew that he was a trooper and that he would come out on top. Once he finished, I felt relived. Just as he walked out, my grandfather walked around the room in a daze. I could tell by the look on his face that he was fighting back tears.

I walked out the room because I needed some air and I needed to check on Nellie. Soon as I walked outside, my phone rung. It saw it was Nique again, so I hit ignore again because I still didn't have time for her shit right now. I had way too much going on to deal with her right now. I walked to my car and grabbed the blunt that I rolled before we left the club. I needed to get this shit under wraps fast. I told the doctor that I wanted them to put in the system that Puff was dead. That way, whoever did this would come for me next, and I was going to catch they ass. One thing was for sure, they were going to try me next, and I was going to be waiting.

2 NELLIE

$\mathcal{I}$ was in so much pain and the fact that these damn officers where asking me the same damn questions over and over didn't help. " Look I told you that I didn't see anything. Can please leave my head is hurting and I need to get some rest," I damn near yelled. Peaches was still on the other said of the room just looking. I could tell that she was trying to keep from saying something to them. They had been in here three damn times and each time they got the same damn reply. It was two officers one was a female and the other was a male. The male was just standing back while the female talked. I could tell that she was getting mad because I wouldn't tell her anything. Truth is I didn't know who had done this. My only worry was if Puff was ok. All the other shit didn't matter to me. After they saw that I wasn't going to tell them shit they finally left. Words can't describe how happy I was.

"Call Cream and see how Puff is doing," I instructed. I knew that she was probably tired of me but I didn't care. I needed to know that my man was good.

"He said that he's good but see how soon you can be

discharged because they are going to have him moved," she told me with the phone up to her ear.

"Ok, I will ask when they come back in." I wanted to asked more question, but I knew that he wouldn't tell me. I knew that something had to be going on for him to say that. There was no reason for them to keep me here. I had a few scratches but that was about it. I blacked out because of the impact. I hit the nurse button because I knew that it would be awhile before they came back in here, due to the fact that they had just left out.

Peaches came over and got in the bed with me as I waited for the nurse. " I'm so happy that you are ok," she told me. I just smiled because I was happy as well. I just knew that my ass was going to be dead when I felt the car flopping over. I had never been in a car accident, but I had to admit it was scary. I was happy that they didn't call my parents because I didn't want them to have to come here. I knew without a doubt that Clay had someone watching them.

"Don't start with that cry baby shit bitch. I'm good," I assured her.

"Aw so you can be a cry baby and I can't? What kind of shit is that? I can't wait to tell Puff this shit," she joked. Her and Puff swore that I was a big ass cry baby. That wasn't the case though. I was just emotional. I was happy that I was away from Clay and free. Hell that was something to cry about if you asked me.

"How are you feeling?" the nurse asked when she walked in the room.

"I'm good… just wanted to get discharged," I told her. She looked at me like I was crazy, but I didn't care.

"Well the doctor wanted to keep you for a few day just to make sure that everything is good. I can discharge you, but I recommend that you stay," she advised. She wasn't talking about shit. Clay had beat my ass worst than this... I was just fine.

"Can you please just do as I asked?" She nodded and walked out the room. Shortly after, Puff's grandfather walked in the room. He was the finest scary looking man that I had ever seen. They looked just like him. That made me wonder what their mother looked like. Puff didn't talk about her often, so I didn't know much about her.

"Puff is woke. We have to get him moved so I'm going to stay here with you until the nurse come. Just let her know that you want to get discharged," he said, taking a seat.

"I already told her. The police have been up here a million times. I told them I didn't know anything each time, but they just kept coming back so I'm ready to go," I explained. A few minutes later, she came with the discharge papers. It was hell standing up. I was dizzy as hell. Let not talk about the headache that I had. I just wanted to be in a comfortable bed to sleep. When we made it down stair, Pops told us to stay by the door while he went to get his truck. I couldn't help but to feel like someone was watching me. I looked around but didn't see anyone that I knew. I looked at Peaches, but she was too busy in her phone to notice anything. I just shook it off as he pulled to the door. The whole ride to his house, I kept looking back. I just wanted to make sure that no one was following us. That shit had fucked my mind up. We made it to his house in no time. The housekeepers got me comfortable in one of the rooms. Soon as I laid down, my ass was knocked out.

3 PUFF

IN THE MEANTIME IN PUFF'S HOSPITAL ROOM

I was laying in my uncomfortable ass hospital bed. I had been laying there acting like I was still sleep because I didn't want to talk. All I could think about was the fact that someone that we helped eat was trying to kill me. Clay had been copping from us for years. He was a small time nigga that wished that he was big. From what I heard, he was getting a little money in Vegas but nothing to brag about. The only reason that we fucked with that nigga was because his uncle used to work for Pops.

I opened my eye, and there was a nurse in the room, so I hurried and closed them back. I wasn't ready for anyone to know that I was up. I listened as she called someone and told them that I was still alive but on life support. Which was a lie. I waited until I heard her walk out before opening my eyes again. My phone was on the table, so I grabbed it and powered it on. I needed to call my brother. Soon as it powered on, it started ringing. It was a number that I didn't know, so I didn't answer. Once it stopped ringing, I called my brother, and he answered on the first ring. "I'm getting off the elevator," he told me before we ended the call. A few minutes later, he walked into the room.

"It was a nurse in here, find out who she is. She was talking to someone and telling them that I was still alive. Go find that bitch!" I roared. I was so pissed. "And where is Nellie?" Cream gave me a look that I knew all too well. It was the disappointing look. Just as he was getting ready to answer me, his phone rung. He answered but he didn't say anything; he just listened for a second.

"That nigga up, tell her to get discharged. Pops is going to come up there with y'all." Cream said a few more thing to them and then ended the call. I was relived because I knew that she was good. My mind went right to the nurse that was in here. I needed to find out who she was and who she worked for. Cream asked how she looked before walking out the room. A few minutes after he left, Lipz walked in the door. I closed my eyes as fast as I could. I could feel her hovering over me.

"Baby, I'm so happy that you ok. I just came to take care of you," she said, rubbing her hand down my legs. Her touch was so soft. My dick damn near got hard until she opened her mouth again. "Shit," she mumbled as her phone rang.

"Hello….. No bitch, I'm still here…. I'm trying to get his shit now. Mesha said that he was on life support, so he won't know what I'm doing…. I'ma call you back," she told whoever was on the phone. It took everything in me not to jump up and kill her ass. What the hell was she trying to do? My question was answered when she slid her hand under the sheets. This bitch was about to rape me. I prayed that my brother walked in because I didn't want her to know that I was alive. I didn't know who she knew or was working with.

I guess God was listening because my brother walked in just as she was pulling the cover off me. "Yo bitch, what the fuck you doing? Get the fuck out of here before I kill yo nasty ass," Cream hissed. It took everything in me not laugh at his ass. She was dumb as fuck anyway. If I was on life support, I would have been hooked to all kinds of machines, but my ass was laying here not hooked to shit but an IV monitor. Once I heard the door slam, I opened my eyes. We both just busted out laughing.

"Nigga, yo ass was about to get raped... I saved yo life. You owe me for that shit," he joked. " I'm glad it was me walking in and not Nellie or Peaches. Her ass would have been in a bed right next to yo ass," Cream said as he pulled his phone out.

"I gotta get yo ass out of this hospital fast," he laughed. I didn't object because he was telling the truth. He sat next to me while he made the necessary calls. Once he was done, he let me know that Nellie was already gone; I was happy to hear that. I could wait to get to her ass.

A few hours later, the people came to transport me to Pops' house. I was happy to get away from this hospital. There was no telling what else would have happened if I would have stayed longer. Hell, there was no telling when happened when I was knocked out. Soon as I got in the house, I had the housekeeper to go and get Nellie. I needed to see that she was ok myself. She walked into the room and I could see all of the scratches on her body. She was wearing some little ass shorts and a tank. She didn't have on a bra, but her titties were sitting up perfectly.

"Come here," I demanded because she was just standing at the door looking crazy. She made her way to me. Although I was in pain, I needed her to be close to me. She climbed in the bed with me slowly so that she didn't hurt me.

No words needed to be spoken as she laid her head on my chest. We laid there in silence, looking out the window. Just when she thought that I was sleep, Nell kissed me and told me that she loved me. I just kept my eyes closed because I didn't know if I wanted to say it back.

I drifted off to sleep because I had a lot to do when I got up. I was going to see Clay's ass.

4 NIQUE

$\mathcal{I}$ had been calling Cream for two days. I had heard that his brother had been shot. I knew that he was going crazy and that he needed me, so I couldn't understand why he wasn't answering. That bitch that he was fucking with didn't know how to take care of him. I decided that I would just got to the hospital since he wasn't answering for me. One way or the other, he was going to talk to me. Plus, I wanted to know if his brother was alive or not.

When I walked in, I asked the nurse what room Puff was in, and she told me that he had passed. I pulled my phone out to called Cream again. When he didn't answer, I headed to his house. I knew that he had change the gate code, but I also knew that the guard had a thing for me. I pulled up there in no time. I was happy that Stan was there. I parked and walked up to the gate. I made sure to pulled my shirt down so that my prefect breasts were sitting up just right.

"Hey Stan," I cooed. He looked up from his phone and smiled. "I just came to check on Cream. I heard about Puff and I wanted to check on him. Can you let me in the gate? If you do, I got something for you," I said, licking my lips.

"Show me what you got for me first," he said, opening the door to the guard's shed. I walked in and he closed the door behind me, then closed the window. I dropped down to my knees. Cream's ass *better* take me back. I was going through all of this for his ass. When Stan pulled his dick out, my eyes popped out of my head. This old man's dick was so fucking big, hell I didn't think that it was all going to fit in my mouth. That shit was not normal at all. I closed my eyes and prepared for what I needed to do. I imagined that it was Cream's dick that I was sucking so that I wouldn't be creeped out. It took him no time to nut, especially since I was so into it. Once I was done, I opened my eyes to see that he was recording me.

"What the fuck Stan? Why would you record me?" I asked as I got up.

"Shit, why not second this shit so I can get a nut off later?" he said as if what he did was cool.

"Just let me in the gate," I said while looking in my purse for a piece of gum. He didn't reply, so I turned to see him smiling at the phone. I walked out the door and waited for the gate to open. When it didn't after I minute, I walked back to the shed. "Um... are you going to open the gate so that I can go check on him?"

"Aw he ain't here... he left a while ago," Stan said, pissing me off.

"So you let me suck your dick and you knew that he wasn't here?" He just nodded. I was so fucking pissed that I just went to my car. I was going to get into that gate.

I pulled off and headed to my mom's house. The whole ride there, I thought about what I could do to get Cream back. Then it clicked. I was going to use Tez. I headed straight to his house instead. I knew that he had to have some sort of videos or pictures of him and Peaches. I was going to use that to break them up. I pulled into Tez's driveway to see him outside with his baby mama. I waited until she was in her car and gone before I walked up to the door. Soon as he answered, I was walked in. I was happy to see that he was eating some chicken. He knew that was my favorite.

"Where you been? I been calling you," he said when I sat down.

"I was taking care of something for my mama. Didn't you say that Cream's girl was your ex?" I asked, getting straight to the point.

"Yes, why you asked that?"

"Do you have any videos of y'all or any pictures that she sent you? I got a plan to break them up," I advised him. He pulled out his phone and started scrolling. Shortly after, my phone dinged. I looked at the pictures and smiled. Tez leaned over and kissed me. That shit had my pussy dripping. We laid right there on his mama couch and fucked. Just as we were finishing up, the front door opened. I just knew that it was going to be his mother walking in, but then I remembered that she was in Mexico with her boyfriend.

"Damn, can I get some of that good pussy?" His nigga Raye said as he walked all the way in the house. Tez was fucking me from the back so I had a good view of the door. Raye walked in and pulled his dick out just as Tez got his nut. I hadn't done no shit like this since high school. Soon as Tez left and went to the bathroom, Raye came over to me and slid his dick in. It had been years since I let some niggas run a train on me, but I was for it. I loved fucking so I had no problems with it.

Once Raye got his nut, I went to the basement to shower. When I came back up, they were talking about Cream and Puff. I stood to the side so that I could hear them but not be seen.

"Look, since the Puff nigga is dead, all we gotta do is get

close to Cream. You need to use her ass for that shit. She lived with the nigga, so you know she knows where he live and some mo shit. You need to use that ho' to your advantage," Raye told Tez. I wanted to see what his ass was going to say back.

"Shit, she out for they ass to. I slick think that she was trying to get that nigga back. But we gone let her lead us to that nigga," Tez said. I had a trick for the both of them since they thought that they were going to play me. When I get done, I'm going to be the only one standing.

5 CLAY

A FEW DAYS LATER

*N*ique had been acting funny the past few days. I didn't know what was up with her, but I was going to find out. I walked in her room and she was laid across the bed. She was wearing some little ass short that had her ass sitting up right. That shit had my dick getting hard. I adjusted myself before taking a seat on the bed. I knew that she heard me walk in but she didn't turn around.

"What's up baby?" I spoke, pulling her towards me.

"Where you been Clay? I been calling you for two days," she said. When she said that, it reminded me that I had blocked her number because I was laid up with this lil female, and I didn't need them into it and shit.

"I was busy baby. You know a nigga out here getting this money. When I head back home, you rolling with a nigga?" I asked to see were her head was. If she said yes, then I knew that she was for a nigga; if she said no, then I was going to fuck her one last time and dip. I had already killed one of them, so now I just needed to hit Cream were it hurt. And from what I heard, it was that bitch that he was fucking with.

That's where Nique was going to come in. I needed her to break that bitch.

"Baby, you know I'm rolling with you," she said, calling me to smile.

"Good. I need you to do something so we can speed this shit up and get away from here. I need you to come up with a way to end that Peaches bitch. If we do that, it will break Cream. That will make it easier to rob his ass blind. Can you do that for me baby?"

"You know I will do that shit with pleasure," she assured me.

It was on from that point. I had her ass bent over in less than five minutes. Once we were done, we headed out to set our plan on motion. She said that since his brother was killed, Cream was going to have Peaches on lockdown, but we knew that she was going to have to come out. We pulled up to the nigga's house and she parked across the street and waited. I didn't care how long it took, I was going to get their asses.

* * *

THREE DAYS HAD PASSED and there was no movement at the house outside of the guards, so we decided to go and let shit die down and come back full force. Besides, I needed to go home and get a team together. The whole plane ride back to Vegas, Nique went on and on about the Peaches bitch while I was worried about Amber. It was like she disappeared. When I heard that she didn't die, I went to the hospital but she wasn't there. It didn't even show in the system that she had been there. When I first got home, I rode past her parents' spot. I didn't approach them because they had a restraining order on me, and I didn't need them calling the police on my ass because they were known for that. If I knew Amber, she wouldn't be calling them anyway. They hated our relationship so that put a wedge in theirs.

I walked into the bedroom and Nique was wearing Amber's robe. That shit pissed me off because I told Nique not to wear her shit. Now don't get me wrong, she looked good as fuck in it, but it was still the fact that it wasn't hers.

"What I tell you?" I asked as I kicked my shoes off. She just looked at me and took the robe off. All that anger I had instantly left. She was ass naked. Nique was a stone cold freak. She was ready to fuck whoever and whenever. I wished Amber was like that; Nique had a nigga's pockets fat. Hell, we had only been here a few weeks and she had already made me more money than I made selling dope. She sold her shit to the highest bidder. The crazy thing was, I didn't ask her to do it.

She dropped to her knees and pulled my joggers down on the way. She was sucking my shit so good that I couldn't answer my ringing phone. "What up?" I managed to get out.

"Them nigga sent some nigga down here to look for you," my nigga Pat said. When he said that, I looked down at Nique and wanted to stop her but couldn't. At the same time, I was trying not to moan in this nigga's ear.

"Aite," was all that I could get out before hanging up. I let her do her thang then headed back out. I needed to go and see what was up with them niggas sending niggas at me.

"Don't open this door for anyone," I told her. Nique nodded and walked into the bathroom. On the way out the house, I made sure to cut everything off. If I knew her, she was about to go to sleep… that's all her ass did. I guess it was because she didn't really know anyone here other than her clients.

When I pulled on the block, it was popping. There was people everywhere. I sat there for a second so that I could peep what all was going on and to make sure there were no new faces. Once I felt that I was good, I got out the car. Just as I did, Pat walked over to me.

"What's good nigga? I didn't think you would come out," he said, damn near pissing me off. Why would he think that? I wasn't finna let no nigga run me from where I run shit. This was *my* block. Everyone knew who Cream and Puff were. Most of these niggas was scared of them, but I wasn't. I ended Puff's life, so Cream needed to be easy. I had my ears to the street, so I knew that Cream had no idea that it was me that killed his brother. He thought that it was some beef shit. I wanted it to stay that way to. Just as that thought left my mind, Nique called. I knew that she didn't want shit, so I hit ignore. I needed to get my shit together so that I could go back and take over. I needed to get at them niggas asap. Like within the next few days.

6 PEACHES

TWO WEEKS LATER

"*B*aby, can you please come and get this box down?"
I yelled through the house. I was getting out the
decorations that his housekeeper had stored away. I loved
fall and couldn't wait to see what all stuff he had. I had to do
something to keep myself busy. I was starting to feel alone,
especially since he had been through so much. Some days, he
was here all day and other days, he wasn't here until it was
time to go to bed. It had been this way since Puff had gotten
shot. He had Puff at their grandfather's house, so most time,
that's where he was. I was happy that I at least had Nellie.
When she wasn't hid out with Puff, she was here.

"Nah, we can do that later... we finna go to Pops' house,"
he told me. I was happy because I was ready to get out the
house. Plus, I missed Nell. I rushed to the room so that I
could get dressed. Since it was getting cold, I decided on
some ripped jean and Gucci t-shirt with the matching shoes.
I grabbed my purse and we headed out the door.

"Damn, them jeans got that ass looking good baby,"
Cream said as we made our way to the car. My ass was
blushing like a high school girl. Cream was more than I could

ask for in a man. If you would have told me that I would be with him a year ago, I would have laughed in your face. He was so far from my type that it was scary. I always tried to stay away from street niggas. Tez tried to act street, but he was really square as hell. He came from a good home and went to private school until he was in the tenth grade. He just played the role so that he could fit in.

"Baby, did you check on the school stuff?" Cream asked as he pulled out of the back drive way. Since Puff got shot, we had been going out the back drive way. No one knew about it but him, Puff, and now me.

"Yep, I have it written down at the house. Classes start in a few weeks... I just forgot to tell you about it."

"Ok good. I also want you to think about a business that you would want to open." I just nodded and smiled. Like I said before, he was the perfect man for me.

"Ok, I will let you know baby. Have you talked to your mother?" I asked. That was a touchy subject, but it was one that needed to be addressed. He looked over at me and then focused back on the road. I knew what silence meant so I didn't push the issue. I knew that when he was ready to talk, he would. When Puff got shot, she didn't come around at all. She didn't even call and check on him. I knew that hurt Puff more so than anything because he was rooting for his mom. It took us no time to get to his grandfather's house.

"I will call her baby, I promise. I'm just not ready yet. Have you talked to your mother ?" He asked. Cream knew damn well that I hadn't talked to her ass. I had no desire to talk to her ass. I got out the car without saying shit to his ass. He knew the answer, so I was not going to waste my time answering.

I walked ahead of him. I knew that he was looking at my ass, so I made sure that I walked hard, jiggling just like he liked it. I walked in to see Nellie laid out on the couch. If I didn't know better, I would think that her ass was pregnant. All she did was sleep and eat.

"What's good sis?" Puff asked as he came from the kitchen.

"Nothing. Puff, let me find out you don't knocked her ass up." That nigga's head turned so damn fast. I laughed so damn hard. Nellie's ass was looking like a deer pinned in headlights. I wanted to comment but I changed my mind. I was going to let her live for now.

"Says the bitch that haven't had a period..." she blurted. I damn near choked and I wasn't drinking shit. I wanted to kill her ass. That shit pissed me off but that's what my ass get. Both Cream and Puff just walked out the room. I wanted to go right behind them, but I needed to curse her ass out first. I looked around the corner to make sure that they were gone before walking over and pushing her talking ass.

"Bitch, why the fuck would you do that?" I asked.

"Same damn reason why you did it to me bitch. Don't think that you can do that shit to me and I let it roll. Now bitch, you need to be taking this test," she said, pulling a Walgreens' bag from under her. For the past few weeks, I haven't been feeling good. It had been hell hiding it from his ass. I didn't want him to think that I was trying to trap him, so I wanted to know for sure before I told him. We really never talked about kids, so I didn't know where he stood on them.

I took the bag and went to the bathroom. Apart of me was scared then there was this part that was happy. I wanted a baby, but I didn't want to be like my mother. I wanted to be a good mother. I pulled the test out of the box before pulling my pants down. I sat down and urinated on the stick before sitting it on the counter. I cleaned myself, washed my hands, and hopped up on the sink. I didn't want to take a chance to leave out and someone came in behind me.

I set the timer on my phone and started scrolling on Instagram. I clicked on a message that was from a user that was not following me. I knew that it was Nique's hoe ass. She had been fucking with me for the longest. It was ok because I was going to get a chance to beat her ass.

The time went off just as there was a knock at the bathroom door. "Hold on," I shouted at whoever was at the door. I knew that it was Nellie's nosey ass. I looked at the test and was stuck. I was about to be someone's mother.

"Yo, what the fuck you doing in there?" Cream yelled through the door. Soon as I heard his voice, worry washed over me.

"Umm... here I come baby. I had too shit, damn," I lied. I wrapped the test in some tissue and stucked that and the Walgreens' bag deep in my purse before opening the bathroom door. He was standing there on his phone as always. I just walked passed his ass.

"So you just gone walk past me?" Cream asked, putting his phone in his pocket.

"Shit, I thought yo ass needed to use the bathroom the way that you was knocking on the door," I said with an attitude. I was in my feelings and didn't want to talk and he was with the shit. He just wanted to see what I was doing as if I wasn't allowed to go in the bathroom for a long period of time. Hell, when his ass shitted, he was in the damn bathroom for damn near thirty minutes.

"What's up with this attitude, shit? You been on some other shit all fucking week. You got something you need to get off yo mind?"

"No," was all I said as I walked pass his ass. I ambled to the living room and took a seat next to Nellie. I knew that she was anxious to ask me what the test said but both of their nosey ass were in the room. I was ready for Pops to come downstairs, so they ass could go in another room.

"So bitch, what did it say?" Nellie asked soon as they were gone. I pulled it out of my purse and handed into her. She smiled so big. "I'm so happy that our babies are going to pop up together," she beamed. I had to do a double take.

"Bitch, you pregnant and didn't tell me?" I asked, although I knew because she was getting bigger and all her ass did was sleep and eat.

"Yes, I took the other test that was in the box… that's why there was only one in the box," she told me. That made me a little happier, but honestly, I didn't know if I was ready to be a mother as I said before.

7 PUFF

I didn't know what was up with Nellie and Peaches but I was going to find out soon. I was going to wait until Nellie thought that I forgot and bring it back up. I had been thinking that she was pregnant, but she hadn't said shit to me. I didn't think that I was ready for a baby, but if we got blessed with one, then I was all for it.

"Pops' ass needs to come on. I got shit to do," Cream said. That nigga's ass was lying; he didn't have shit to do. He was just pissed at Peaches so he was ready to go home. Just as he said that, Pops came downstairs with Ms. Rose following behind.

He spoke to Peaches and headed to his office. We both got up and followed. I was the last to walk in, so I closed the door behind me. I sat down and so did Cream. I was happy that I was able to get around now. God was with me because I was supposed to be dead. That nigga shot me at point blank range. I couldn't wait to get a hold of that Clay nigga. I had sent some nigga to bring his ass to me, but they said the nigga hadn't been around. I was going to get his ass one way or the other. I don't care if I had to go to Vegas to get his ass myself.

"Have you heard from Nique?" Pops asked Cream as he lit a blunt.

"Nah, the bitch not answering for me. I went by her mama's house and she claimed that she had talked to her. I knew that shit was a lie," Cream explained. Someone told us that they saw Clay and Nique together, so we knew that she had something to do with me damn near being killed. I had been telling my brother than hoe was no good.

"Ok, so we also need to be looking at that nigga that be with Scale. Ray or whatever his name is. I been hearing that he been talking slick and been hanging with the nigga that Peaches was fucking with," Pops advised. I didn't know much about the nigga that she used to fuck with, but I was more than sure that Cream was going to find out all that we needed to know. The only thing that I did know was that the nigga had gotten her best friend pregnant.

"Y'all need to handle that... I will keep my eyes and ears out for the Clay nigga. He know that he owes y'all, so he is going to been looking for somebody to cop from. I already put the word out so when he tries, we're going to get his ass," Pops told us. I couldn't wait to get his ass. We talked about a few other things then Cream headed out so that he could go and check the progress on the condos. Once they were gone, I sat next to Nellie. I could tell that she was unconformable because she kept moving.

"So you pregnant?" I asked. I wanted to see if she was going to tell me or was I going to have to force her to tell me. She just looked at me like I was crazy.

"Puff, don't be listening to Peaches ass," she said before getting up. I knew that she thought that I was just going leave it alone but I wasn't. I called my Pops ' housekeeper and told her to go to Walgreens and get a few test. Since she wanted to play, I was going find out myself. I looked up to see her going upstairs. I didn't say a word. I just sat there. I was so damn tired of being in this house. I was waiting till I got that nigga before I show my face.

I just walked off because I was going to find out what I needed to know one way or the other. I went to chill till the housekeeper came back with what I needed. It took almost an hour before she came back. When she did, I headed to the room that we had been sleeping in. Nellie was laid across the bed reading a book. I was starting to think that her and Peaches were in a competition. All they did was read then call each other and talk about it.

"Get up," I demanded. Nell didn't move so I repeated myself, although that was something that I hated doing. This time, she turned toward me but still didn't get up. We had been together long enough for her to know how I felt about her not doing what I asked.

"What is it Donald?" she asked as if I was getting on her nerves.

" Need you to take these," I said, throwing the bag on the bed. Nellie looked down at the bag then turned back to her book that she was reading. I took a deep breath because she was pissing me off.

"Nellie, you can get up and take them or I can make you, it your choice," I told her before walking out of the room. She was a grown ass woman. I shouldn't have to beg her to do shit that she knew that she needed to do. I went to talk to Pops for a minute so that I could calm down.

"What's up son?" Pops greeted me as I walked into his office.

"Nothing. Nellie about to make me kill her ass," I told him. He looked at me and started laughing. He loved Peaches and Nellie. In his eyes, they were for us.

"What she do?" he asked.

"I think she's pregnant but she acting like she don't want to take a test to see," I fussed.

"How did you approach her? You know how you not good at talking to people." Just as he said that, my phone rung. That was odd because everyone thought that I was dead, so no one should have been calling me. Both me and my grandfather looked at the phone.

"Who the fuck could that be?" he asked. I just shrugged. We both just brushed it off and continued with our conversation.

8 CREAM

"So you gone tell me what's up with you?" I asked Peaches as soon as we walked in the house. She just kept walking as if I hadn't said shit to her. "Yo, I know you fucking hear me Tianna?" I yelled, grabbing her by her arm. She was tripping hard. We had been together for nearly a year and this was the first time that we had argued like this. Normally, we just said what we had to say and moved on.

"I said that I was good," she snatched away and stomped up the stairs. I wanted to go behind her but I had shit to handle. I just grabbed my keys and headed out the door. I would deal with her later.

I jumped in my car and headed to the trap. So much had been going on that I hadn't really been there. I had been letting Scale handle everything for me. He called earlier to tell me that niggas were thinking that since I hadn't been around, they could do what they wanted. He said that he had to kill at least five niggas in past few weeks. I needed to show these niggas that shit was still the same. They thought since my brother was gone, that shit was going change, but they had another thing coming if they thought that.

I sat outside for awhile so that I could see what was going on. It didn't seem too bad, so that meant that Scale was keeping shit in line. I got out the car and headed to the door. When I walked in, it was clean as expected. Scale walked to the front with his gun aimed. He saw that it was me so he put his gun down.

"What's up nigga? Yo ass damn near got popped," he joked.

"Shit, I need to come and show my face for a minute," I told him. He nodded and we both walked to the back of the house. He was counting money so I joined in. He had been doing everything for the past month, but I was going to step in and start back helping.

"When the last time you talked to that ho' Nique?" Scale asked.

"Nah, I'm straight on that ho'. I been hearing shit about her tho. I need to hit the ho' up so that I can keep her close because her days are coming to an end," I assured him. He was just like my brother when it came to Nique; he couldn't stand her ass. We sat and did count twice before putting it all away. When we did count, we sent everyone out. The only people who knew where we kept money was me, my brother, and Scale. That way, if anything happened, we knew where to look. Just as we finished, this nigga that worked for us name Dre strolled in the door. He was a young nigga and was all about his money.

"What's good Boss Man?" he greeted me. "Haven't seen you around. How you been holding up?"

"I been as good as I can. Just taking shit one day at a time." Dre just nodded and headed to the back.

"That little nigga all about his money," Scale told me. " Hell, he the only one that hadn't be with the shit. I had to off Jay and Ken ass. So he been working this alone. I need to get someone else here with him, but in the mean time, I been here," Scale told me. I just nodded to let him know that I understood what he was saying. I was going to keep a eye on Dre so that I could promote him if needed. I took a seat on the couch and just watched him for a while. He worked well and the fiends loved him. One thing that I did love was that he wasn't one of them niggas that let the fiend pay with bullshit. He went finking with them if they didn't have money in hand. The one time that he did, he brought some diapers and then they paid him with the money. That was how I liked it. When you let them pay with other shit, money didn't add up. You ended up losing more than you made because that was not shit that you actually needed.

The thing that Dre did that I didn't like was having his girl and baby pull up. That was a big no-no. I waited until they were gone before I pulled him to the side and talked to him. I had Scale to call someone else over to work for him for a while. I wanted to talk to him and see where his mind was at.

"Aye Dre, come ride with me," I said as I sauntered towards the door. He got up and came behind me. Once we were in the car, I headed to the hotel. I hadn't been there in a while so I wanted to check in. When I walked in, Tisha gave me a head nod since she was with a customer. We headed to the restaurant. I strolled right to my normal table. Tanya walked up and hugged me. I will be so happy when all this shit was over with and when Puff came out of hiding because I was over people feeling bad for me. Sometimes, I had to catch myself because I wanted to tell them that I was good and so was he.

"So where do you see yourself in five years?"

When I asked that, Dre sat his phone down and looked at me. "I want to be in your position. I don't want to have to work for anyone. I want to be able to enroll my daughter in a good school and give her everything that I didn't have. That's my sole goal and all that I want," he told me. I just nodded. We needed someone that could step up because after all of this shit was over, I was stepping back and letting Scale run this place. He just had to have someone else in other than Raye. I didn't trust that nigga. I had been hearing shit in the streets, so there was no way that he was getting a hand on my shit.

"I been watching you. I see and like the way that you work. One thing that I will say that I didn't like was that you had yo girl and baby coming to the trap. Always remember the more money that you get, the more niggas gone hate. Keep ya family private. That why when niggas are trying to get to you, they won't go through them," I schooled him. We talked about a few other things while we ate then headed back to the trap. Once I dropped him off, I headed home.

When I got to the house, I sat there for a second because I knew that I needed to get my mind together before dealing with Peaches' ass. It was like her attitude was getting worst by the day. I walked in to see her on the couch looking crazy. The TV was off and so were all of the lights except the lamp when you walk in the door. I took my shoes off and marched over to her. She hated for people to come in the house with shoes on. Since she had been here, Peaches had redone the whole damn house. It looked nothing like the way that it did when Nique was here. She even made me buy new beds.

"Are you ready to talk Tianna?" I asked, calling her by her real name. That way, she would know that I was dead ass serious.

"Donavan," she pleaded. I didn't want to hear that shit.

"I'm listening." It looked like she was about to cry and that alarmed me. I hadn't really said shit to her crazy ass.

"I can't do this," she said, getting up and running out of the room. I stood there confused as hell. *What the hell just happened?*

I walked around the house until I found her in the back yard. She was sitting on the edge of the pool with her feet in it. I sat next to her and pulled her close to me. I didn't know what was going on with her, but I was worried because I never seen her like this.

"Baby, talk to me... tell me what's wrong so that we can fix it," I pleaded with her. She looked up and I swore that I felled in love all over again. This girl had my ass wrapped around her finger and she didn't even know it.

"We can't fix it."

"Everything can be fix, so just tell me what it is so that we can, baby. This is not you, baby. I need my happy baby back," I told her. She was still looking down at the water.

"I'm pregnant," she blurted. I just looked at her before smiling. When she looked back up at me and saw that I was smiling, her whole facial expression had changed. "You not mad at me?" she asked. Now it was time for me to look at her like she was crazy.

"Mad for what? I been trying to get yo ass pregnant since the first time we fucked," I admitted. She smiled so big. I was calm on the outside but on the inside, a nigga was doing flips. I was happy as hell. I was ready to be a father and have someone to pass my legacy on to.

9 NELLIE

*P*uff made my ass hurt some damn times. He always felt that he ran me. I dealt with controlling shit with Clay, so I was not going to deal with it with his ass. He knew how I felt about that shit. I didn't want to take the test because I knew that I was indeed pregnant. I had taken a test a week ago. That's how I was able to give Peaches a test. I just didn't know if I wanted to tell him right now. I needed time to let it sink in. I also wanted to tell my mother first, but I now knew that wasn't going happen. I laid in the bed and read my book until he came back into the room. I knew that he was going to be mad when he came in and saw that the bag was still where he left it.

"Nellie, what did I tell you?" He said, marching in the room. I wanted to laugh so hard because I knew that he was mad. I didn't have to look at him because it was all in his voice.

" Don't have to do shit. I keep telling you that you need to stop bossing me around. I'm grown and I don't do shit that I don't want to do. Now get out my face with that shit," I said before looking back at my phone. I hated that shit.

"Yo, who the fuck you talking to?" Puff said, walking closer to me.

"Yo ass getting on my nerves. I'm not taking that shit... you fucking take them, shit," I said, getting up from the bed. He had me fucked up—that made me mad that damn fast. I walked to the closet so that I could get me something to put on when I got out the shower. I grabbed my clothes and headed to the bathroom. I closed the door behind me because I didn't want to deal with his nagging ass. Just as I was getting in the shower, he bust in. I rolled my eyes even though he couldn't see me. Puff was so used to running shit that he thought he was going to run me and that wasn't happening. I continued to shower as if his ass wasn't in the bathroom. I got out the shower and slipped my clothes on after I put on some lotion. His ass was just sitting there looking crazy. I acted like I didn't even see his ass. Once I was done, I headed back to the room.

"So fuck what I said, huh?" I think part of me didn't want to tell him because I didn't know if I could carry a baby. I had been pregnant by Clay twice. I didn't know if he beat the baby out of me or I just lost it. Either way, I didn't want to bring that kind of pain on Puff. So I was going wait until I went to the doctor before telling him.

"Puff, please get out my face."

"You wanna act tough and shit, you should have been acting like this when that nigga was beating yo ass," he yelled, causing me to turn and look at him. I couldn't believe he said that shit. Before I knew it, tears were forming in my eyes.

"You know what? Fuck you, Puff! I don't have time for this shit. You right, I should have been like this with him. I'm gone so that way, you don't have to worry about me being tough," I said, grabbing my purse and phone. I was doing everything I could to keep the tears from rolling.

"Where you going Nellie?" Puff asked as he trotted behind

me. I didn't have shit to say to his ass. "Nellie, you really finna leave?" Puff asked like he couldn't really believe that I was leaving. I wanted to kick his big ass house, but I just walked out the door. Once I made it outside, I opened my Uber app and called me a Uber. The app said that I had ten minutes, so I used that time to call Peaches, letting her know that I was on the way.

"Hey boo," she happily greeted me. I knew that she had to have told Cream that she was pregnant because she was pissed when she left Pops' house.

"I'm on my way there," I told her. I guess she could hear it in my voice that something was wrong because that was her next question. I gave her a brief run down and we ended the call. I think the part that bothered me the most was that he didn't even come and see if I was gone or shit.

When my Uber pulled up, I headed to the gate because I knew that they wouldn't let the car in. The whole way to Peaches' house, I cried. How could Puff say something like that to me? That showed me that he didn't give a fuck about my feelings. Damn, that was some fucked up shit to say, knowing what I had been through.

"Hey, can you stop at the store right here?" I asked the driver. He just nodded and pulled on the gas station lot. I got out and headed into the store. I just wanted to get me some snacks. I grabbed what I needed and headed to the counter. Once I was done paying for my stuff, I headed back to the Uber. I damn near died when I walked out the door and saw Clay leaning up against the Uber. How the fuck did he find me? I been in hiding just so that he wouldn't find me. I tried backing back into the store, but it was just my luck that the door didn't work like that.

"Umm... Clay, what are you doing here?" I asked as if I didn't know the answer.

"Let's go," was all that he said. I looked in the car at the driver with pleading eyes. I needed him to save me. I knew that he wouldn't when the driver pulled off. I looked around to see if I could run but that wasn't happening because there was nowhere to go. I slowly walked towards him. I couldn't call anyone because my phone was in my pocket. When I made it to him, Clay pushed me into the car before going to the driver's side and getting in. I tugged on the door, but he had the child lock on so I couldn't get out. I even tried letting down the window, but it wouldn't come down either. I knew at that moment that I was fucked. The whole ride to wherever we were going, he didn't say a word. We pulled up at house, but I didn't really see anything that would make a difference. Clay opened the door for me to get out and grabbed my purse. I was not happy that he searched me because I still would had my phone. When we walked in the house, we went down some stairs into a basement.

"Clay, why are you doing this?" I asked. He didn't reply; instead, he just pushed me on the dirty mattress and walked back out. I just wanted to fucking die. I was pissed at myself because I was being stubborn and now my ass was kidnapped. I could have easily just went into one of the many rooms in Pops' house, but my dumb ass didn't and look at me now.

10 PUFF

*N*ellie was on some other shit. I wanted to go after her, but I couldn't be seen. I didn't know who was watching. I just stood at the door to make sure that she got in the Uber. When she pulled off, I called my brother to tell him that she was on the way. I knew that was the only place that she would go. Nellie brought feelings out of me that I didn't know that I could have for a female. Hell, she had a nigga in love. That was new for me. I was the type of nigga that didn't do that love shit. I was about getting what I wanted and dipping. I couldn't name a time that I let a female got so close to me.

I decided to take a shower while I waited on my brother to call and let me know when she made it. After I showered, I noticed that I didn't have miss call from him. Just as I was about to dial his number, my phone rang.

"Nigga, she must changed her mind?" Cream said as soon as I answered.

"Nah, what you talking about? She should have been there by now," I said as I slipped on some pants. Nellie had been gone for damn near an hour and he lived only fifteen minutes away. I pulled out my other pone and dialed her number. I didn't get an answer.

"Have Peaches to call her."

"I have been calling," Peaches said in the background. When she said, that a uneasy feeling came over me. I jumped up and ran to Pops' office. He was looking at something on his computer when I walked in. I guess he could see the worried look on my face because he jumped up from his seat.

"Nellie left an hour ago and now she not answering her phone," I told him. He picked his phone up and started making calls. I called her phone once more from my other number. Apart of me knew that Nell wasn't just ignoring me because she didn't know this number.

"Who did she leave with?" Pops asked as he rolled the cameras back. We watched together as she got into the car with the driver. Pops gave someone the Uber driver's tag number to someone on the phone. I called her phone back to back. I needed to find her. I knew that I was supposed to be in hiding, but I was about to show my face.

"Bring Peaches here... we got to hit the streets," I told him before ending the call. I sat and thought about what the hell could have happen that fast. It didn't take my brother anytime to get here. When he got here, we headed out. There wasn't much on the way to his house but a gas station. Then, I thought about the fact that she love those Rap Snacks that they sold there. So that was our first stop.

"Have you seen her?" I asked the girl behind the counter.

"Yes, she was just here," she told me. Then she offered to roll the cameras back. When I saw that Clay was the one that had her, rage filled my body. That nigga was testing me, so I was finna give him what he wanted.

"I know where to find that nigga. Hit Scale up and tell him to meet us there," Cream said as he jumped in the driver's seat of my truck. I just got in and laid my head back.

I was *fucked*. I shouldn't have said that shit to her. Honestly, that was some fucked up shit to say to her. A nigga was just mad. I called Scale and he told me that he was on the way. I didn't get a chance to tell him what was going on, but he was my nigga, so I knew that he was going to roll no matter what. Hell, he was the only nigga that knew my ass wasn't dead.

We pulled up at Nique's house and we both jumped out. We was going to find her and Nique was going to lead us to Nellie. Cream didn't even knock on the door; he just kicked the door down. I walked in just as Scale and some other nigga pulled up.

"What are you doing in my house?" her mom asked. No one replied; we just walked though the house. No one was there, but I knew that Nique had been there because her luggage was in one of the rooms.

"Where is Nique?" Cream asked. He mother looked like she was going to shit on herself.

"I know yo old ass can hear," I gritted.

"She not here. She left earlier," she cried. We just walked out the door. One thing we knew was that her bitch ass boyfriend was going to come looking for us, and I was going to be ready. The next stop was the trap. We needed everyone to know that I was alive and that I was looking for Clay and his whole crew. What better way to do that than to show my face at the trap.

When we pulled up, one of the niggas that worked for Scale was sitting on the porch. Soon as he saw me, his eyes got big. "Damn nigga, you done came back from the dead?" he asked, causing us all to laugh. The crazy thing was, people should have known that I wasn't dead. There was no funeral or shit; they just heard that I was dead and ran with it.

"Some like that. What's the word on that nigga Clay?" I asked. I knew that he was always in the streets so he would know.

"I heard the nigga was down here looking for some female. Word is she was with you. The nigga left for a while but now he's back. He brought a few nigga with him, but I haven't really seen any of them. You need me to get at the nigga?" he asked.

"Bring me that nigga and I got fifty stack fa ya," I told him before walking in the house. He just nodded and walked off. When we walked in the house, Cream's phone rang. I heard Peaches' voice, so I headed to the back of the house.

11 NELLIE

"So you though that you would just get away, huh?" Clay asked as he paced the small room that I was in. I had been in this damn room for at least three days. I was in so much pain but I would never let him know that. He had been coming in here trying to talk to me, but I hadn't said a word. I didn't have shit to say to his abusive ass.

"So you gone act like you don't hear me talking to you?" he angrily asked. I knew that he was about to knock my ass out soon, but I didn't care at this point. I was more than sure that my ankle was broke.

"You know how much I love you. Why would you just leave like that? Damn, you love that nigga more than you love me?" he asked as if I was going to answer. I closed my eyes and laid my head back as I tried to shift my swollen ankle. He had snatched me so damn hard that I twisted it. Clay knew what made me leave; he knew why I wasn't talking to him. He had damn near killed me because I told him that I didn't want him to stick his dick in my ass. I was convinced that he was gay. Who would get mad about that? I guess them three years he did in jail changed him. I met him when I was fifteen. I just knew that he was all that I would ever want. He was there when my mother got sick as well as when my father was killed.

He made sure that I had everything that I needed. When I turned eighteen, I found out that I was pregnant with my first child. Clay didn't want kids, so he beat the baby out of me. That was the umpteenth time that he hit me. I stayed in the hospital for two weeks. I took his ass back like a fool, and after that, he beat my ass every chance that he got. I went through five pregnancies. The last one, I hid until I was five months. I lost my daughter the day that he tried to have anal sex with me. That was my breaking point. I was *done*. I had to get away from his ass.

"So you not going to talk? I bet this will make you talk," he yelled before kicking my ankle so hard that I was sure that my shit will never be the same. I screamed out so loud that I was sure that the neighbors could hear me. If I made it through this, I was going to kill his ass. I straightened my face up and took a deep breath. Just as he was about to kick my shit again, another guy strolled into the room. I was so damn happy because a bitch couldn't take another hit.

"Aye, let me talk to you for a second," the guy said. Damn I was relived. I needed a minute to get my shit together, hell. I needed to think of a way to get out of here. Hell, the hardest part was going to be walking. There was no way that I could walk on this ankle.

I did my best to hear what they were saying but I couldn't. I laid back, pulling my foot up on the bed. I had to protect my ankle. It was turning blue, so I knew that I was fucked. I was scanning the room for ideas on getting out of here when my eyes landed on a phone. I knew that it wasn't Clay's phone because he had an iPhone. I laid there and listened for a while. I could hear them in the next room. I wanted to give it a little more time before I tried getting up. I needed to make sure that they were gone.

As I laid there, I thought about Puff and wondered if he realized that I was missing. I knew that they would notice soon and hopefully come looking for me. I just wanted to be in his arms. I hated the way that I left because if I didn't make it, it would kill him.

I laid there listening to what all I could hear. The footsteps were moving from the room, so I used all the strength that I had to get up and get the phone. It was a old flip phone. I was happy when I noticed that it was charged. I dialed Peaches' number since that was the only number that I knew by heart. The phone rung and I cut the volume down. That way, if they walked in and I had to hide it, they wouldn't hear it. I made my way back to the bed that I had been laying on and waited for her to answer.

"Hello," she answered, sounding like she was crying.

"Peaches," I whispered.

"Oh my God Nellie! You're alive," she cried. It took everything in me not to do the same. I was so happy to hear her voice.

"Yes I'm ok. Listen, I don't know where they have me, but I know that I'm in a house. My crazy ass ex is here," I finished.

"We all have been calling you. I'm going to go and tell Pops that this is you calling... Puff is going crazy," she told me. I was happy to know that they were looking for me. I had to contain my happiness because if Clay noticed any change in me, then he would use it to his advantage. I was going to ask her a few more things, but I heard him coming back.

"I gotta go," I said, ending the call just in time. I powered the phone off and placed it under the dirty mattress that I was laying on. I laid back just as I was before he walked out the room. When he came back in, Clay sat in the same chair that he was seated in before leaving. He was watching me like a hawk. I knew he thought that I was going break and give in like normal, but that wasn't going to happen. I was going to get out of this one way or another. Clay had made my life a living hell, and I was going to do the same to him one day. I never wanted someone dead so damn bad in my life.

I knew that he would find me, but I just didn't think it would be so soon. Clay was a evil man. I don't know how I didn't see that shit for the jump. I guess his ass played the role good. He wined and dined my ass. He took me on trips and all. Shit changed the day that I told him ass that I loved him. A few days after that, he started beating my ass.

"You been giving that nigga my pussy?" Clay asked, ending the silence in the room. What his ass didn't know was that this was no longer *his* pussy. Puff had written his name all over my shit. That nigga's dick game had me strung out like a motherfucker. Hell for a long time, I thought that Clay had the best but boy was I wrong. Puff had a bitch out here ready to fuck in the middle of the mall parking lot during tax time. Just the damn thought made me smile... that is until that nigga's fist connected with my face. Blood seeped from my mouth, bringing me back to reality. I looked at him and wanted to kill his ass.

"Amber, I know fucking well you wasn't thinking about that nigga while I was talking to you. I don't know why you want to play with me like I won't knock yo fucking teeth down your throat."

"Clay, so now you can read minds?" I smartly said. I knew that would make him mad but I didn't care. I needed to keep him distracted. I knew that Puff would be here soon. I wished that I could go back in life because I would have never given this nigga the time of day. He dicked me down and my dumb ass felled in love, so I can't blame anyone but myself. I should have left long time ago.

"You know a nigga love you, so why you playing?" I had to laugh because he really thought that what he said made sense. I was starting to think that he was slow or some shit.

"Clay, you don't love me because if you did, you wouldn't treat me the way that you do. When you love someone, you take care of them. You show them that you love them," I cried. I knew that I was showing weakness but I didn't care. I thought this man really loved me, but it all was a lie.

"I made sure that you had everything that you needed. I took care of you, so I don't know what you mean."

"What do you call taking care of me? Money is not important... you beat my ass more times than I can count. You cheated on me more times than I can count, and now you want to make it seem like you were good to me when you wasn't. You just want to have someone to control, and I don't want that. I want to enjoy being young and having fun. I can't do that if I always got a damn black eye!" I yelled. I knew that if someone else was here, they would have heard me. I was so loud that my head started hurting.

"Baby, I'm sorry. If you say that you will forgive me, I will change. I just need you baby. Just come home," he pleaded. I didn't love him anymore, so there was nothing that he could say to change that.

"Clay, we both know that you're not going to change. So you might as well kill me now because I'm *not* going back."

He looked at me as if I said something wrong, but I hadn't. That change was only going to be for the moment, plus, I wanted to be here. I had Peaches and Puff. Clay was going to kill my ass, so he may as well do that shit now. He beaten my ass so much that I didn't react to it so that made him madder.

"You coming back," he said before walking out the room. I knew that he was mad as hell, but I didn't care; he would be ok.

12 CLAY

J don't know who Amber thought that she was, but she had me fucked up. She was going back home with me, whether she liked it or not. She was mine and I told her that a long time ago. When she first left, I searched everywhere for her ass but couldn't find her. I was happy the day I got the call from my uncle saying that he saw her and that she was working at some hotel. I followed her for weeks so that I could make sure I caught her at the right time. After following her around, I found out that she was fucking with my connect. I wanted to kill her ass; that's why I got her ass locked in that room now.

That gave me the motive to get him and his bitch ass brother out the way so that I could take over. I knew that sounded like some bitch nigga shit, but it was how I felt.

I sat in the kitchen of this run down house that my uncle owned. I knew that no one would come looking for her because Puff was dead and Cream didn't care that much about her ass.

Now that I think about it, I wished that I would have gotten closer to them; that way, I could have some of the connects that they have, taking them down would be so much easier. I didn't know any of these niggas here and from what I knew, they were loyal to them niggas.

My phone rung, pulling me from my thoughts. I pulled it from my pocket and saw that it was my uncle calling. "Yo," I answered.

"Aye nephew, I need you to meet me. I got some shit brewing. I'm at the spot that we went to the other day," he explained, referring to an old ass building that he said his friend owned.

"Ok, I'm headed that way now," I assured him, getting up from the chair that I was sitting in. I grabbed my gun and headed out the door.

I planned to leave soon then come back and kill Cream's ass. I needed to get Peaches out the way because I knew that they were going to come looking for her. I could tell by the way he looked at Peaches that Cream was in love with her.

On the way to meet my uncle, I decided to call Nique. Her good pussy ass had me thinking about saying fuck Amber's ass. Soon as she answered, I thought about the fact that she was my connection to Cream. She lived with the nigga, so I knew that she knew some shit that could help me take him down.

"What you doing baby?" I asked. I needed to be as nice as I could so that I could get her where I wanted her.

", I'm baby now?" she asked. I could tell that she was smiling. One thing that I knew how to do was charm a female.

"Yea, you baby now. Where you at? Daddy miss you," I lied.

"I'm headed to my mama's house. You on the way here?" she asked. I smiled, thinking about her sucking my dick.

"Yes. I gotta go handle some shit then I'm coming straight to you baby," I assured her. We ended the call and I pulled up to the location that my uncle was at. When I walked in, he was sitting on a box, rolling a blunt.

"So look, I got this lil bitch that said she used to fuck with the Puff nigga. I had her to go to see if the nigga made it. If he didn't, we will have an open window to get Cream since that nigga will be distracted," he explained. I just nodded and pulled out my cigarettes. We talked for a while long then I headed to go buss Nique down while he wasn't there.

When I pulled up to her mother's house, I parked and headed inside the house. My dick was hard just thinking about what she was going to do to me. All that went away when I got on the porch and saw that they door was off the hinges.

"What the fuck happened here?" I asked as I walked in the house. Nique was on the couch with her crying mother. I knew that it had to be Cream, but why would he care this much about Nellie? His brother was gone.

"My mama said that they came and kicked the door down looking for me," Nique cried.

"Who is they?"

"Cream and Puff," she advised. I looked at her ass like she was crazy because Puff was dead—I made sure of that. She then explained that it was indeed the two of them. There was no way that he was still alive. I knew that Nellie was good because my uncle knew the nurse that was assigned to her room when she was in the hospital. I pulled out my phone and called my uncle.

"Get to the house now!" I told him soon as he answered.

"Nigga, who the fuck you think you are calling and demanding that I do some shit?" he smartly replied. See, that was his fucking problem… he didn't know when to shut up and listen. He always had to feel that he was running shit. That's why no one fucked with him. Hell, he told me that he used to work for Cream's grandfather but got cut off. I see why now. I just hung up because I had bigger shit to worry about. I just walked back out the door. He could deal with this shit. I needed to round up the few niggas that I had so that I could get at these niggas before they got at me. Just as I was getting in the car, my phone rang. It was one of the young niggas that I had going to check on the house so I answered.

"What's good?" I answered.

"I'm headed to the house as we speak. I just wanted to keep you updated," is what the young nigga told me. I had him going to sit with Amber because I knew that her ass would try something. Amber was smart as hell. She would make a way out of no way, and I needed her to be there as part of my plan. From what I heard, that bitch that Cream fucked with loved her. That was going to be my bargaining tool. I was gone make that nigga hand over his whole empire.

13 PEACHES

I was so happy to hear from Nellie. I just knew that her ass was dead. I sat on the couch thinking about how dumb her ex had to be in order to leave a phone around her. He probably didn't think that she had the balls to use it. I picked my phone up to call Cream. I had already told Pops that she called and the number that she called from. I just prayed they got to her in time enough.

"What's up baby?" he answered.

"Nellie just called," I told him. Just as he was reeling, Pops walked in and asked for the phone. I handed it to him with no problem. I just wanted to get my friend back safely.

"I tracked the number. I'm sending you the address from my phone now," Pops told him. I felt so relieved because I needed her to be ok. Nellie was all that I had outside of Cream. Shit, my mama wasn't shit so I couldn't lose the love that I had. Speaking of my mother, she had been calling me for the past few days. I wanted to call her but I knew that she was going to be with the shit.

Pops handed me my phone back and walked out the room. I flopped down on the bed and decided to call my mama. I kind of missed her anyway. The phone rang for what seem like forever. "So you finally called back?" I heard the last voice that I wanted to hear answer.

"Tez, why are you answering my mother's phone?" I asked as I sat up on the bed. That made me wonder if that was him constantly calling. "Put my mama on the phone," I demanded. This nigga bussed out laughing.

"Peaches, I told you that I loved you and that Kam was a mistake. I miss you baby. I'm ready for us to get back together," he said as if it made sense. How could he put him fucking my best friend and us getting back together in the same sentence? He could think that I would go for that shit. I was naive sometime time but never dumb.

"Tez, you got my best friend pregnant. What makes you think that I would want to be anywhere near yo ass? Will you just put my mama on the phone? I don't want you. I don't love you. So get over it!" I screamed. He let out a laugh so loud. That made me worry. I prayed that he hadn't done anything to my mother. I didn't think that he would, but I didn't think that he would get my best friend pregnant either. At this point, I didn't put shit passed him.

"Don't worry about ya mama now, you haven't been worried about her. You just need to worry about what you gone wear to that nigga's funeral," he laughed. Before I had a chance to reply, he hung up on my ass. I called the number back, but I didn't get an answer. I just laid back on the bed. I don't think today could get any worse than it already was. I laid there just thinking about my mother, hoping that she could just live right. I wanted to call her phone back, but I didn't know if he had her phone. I couldn't believe that she would give it to him. My mother hated him.

I wanted to call Cream, but I didn't know what he was doing. I prayed that he was somewhere finding Nellie. I wished that she would have just told Puff about her ex; that way, we all could have been protected. I was drifting off to sleep until my phone started ringing. I saw that it was a Facebook call. I sat there debating on if I wanted to answer or not. It was a name that I didn't know so I decided not to answer. The number kept calling; when it finally stopped, I looked the profile up. It had to be Nique because it was a picture of a white girl but the name was ghetto as hell. I was getting tired of her ass. I dialed the number back but didn't get an answer. Just as I hung up, Kam called. What the fuck was going on today? I hit ignore on her ass and laid down.

Kam knew damn well that I wasn't fucking with her. She had crossed me—there was no going back from that. I remember times when she didn't have food to eat. Times when she didn't have a place to stay and I was there. I would never do something like that to her. She was always telling me how I was too good for him, just for her to be fucking him. Then it was like everyone knew but me.

"Hey Ms. Peaches, dinner is ready. Cream told me to make sure you eat," the housekeeper explained. The only reason I got up was because I didn't want her to lose her job because of me. I followed her out the room to see that she had cooked some baked chicken, broccoli, and corn. My stomach started rumbling soon as I laid eyes on the food. Hell, I didn't think that I was hungry. I sat down while she fixed my plate. That was something that I just couldn't get used to. We had a house keeper, but I always told her that she could be off but still made sure that she got paid.

Soon as she sat the plate down, I dugged in. It was so fucking good. I ended up eating two plates full. I still hadn't heard from Cream, so I decided to just lay on the couch. I knew that they would be back soon. I was sleeping good as hell until I heard the front door open. I jumped up and ran to the door.

Puff was carrying Nellie. She was beaten up bad, which

caused me to break down. I was scared for her baby. Soon as he put her down on the couch, I ran over and hugged her. Her eyes were so swollen that you couldn't tell that they were opened. She was worst than she was after the wreck.

"Baby, let the doctor check her out," Cream said, pulling me from my thoughts. I moved out the way so that they could make sure that she was good. I watched as they examined her. I hated that she had to experience this. It was heart breaking.

14 NIQUE

"Where you been?" I asked Tez as he walked through the door. He said that he was going to the gas station hours ago. I was waiting for him to come back because I needed to talk to his ass. I had been gone for a minute and had been hearing that he had been around the city with his baby mama. Granted, I was with Clay but he didn't know that.

"I got a call while I was out, ok," was all he said before going in the kitchen. I could tell that he was mad but I didn't care. I told him that we needed to talk before he left. His ass had been gone all damn day. I knew that he was probably out following his ex that he couldn't seem to get over. Tez didn't tell me much about her, but he did tell me that he had fucked her best friend and got her pregnant. Let's talk about the baby mama. That bitch felt like the world was all about her. What she didn't know was that karma was going to eat her ass up. I have done some fucked u shit, but I never fucked one of my home girls' nigga. That shit was foul as hell.

"I know yo ass lying but whatever." I went to my room so

70

that I could get my phone. I wanted to fuck with Peaches. I logged on the fake page that I made then searched her name. When it pulled up, I saw that she had been out shopping. I knew that Cream had funded that shopping trip. I remember them days; he would just give me his card and I would shop till I dropped.

After I stalked her for a while, I got undressed. I needed to shower anyway. I rolled me a blunt and headed to the shower. I hated taking a shower here because his bathroom was so damn nasty. His ass never cleaned up. I wasn't the cleanest person but I made sure that shit was in order. I just needed Tez to do better. I slipped on my slides that I got from Old Navy then stepped in the shower. I let the hot water rain down on my body. It felt so good. Once I felt that I was clean enough, I stepped out the shower. Soon as I opened the bed room door, I heard Tez and a female arguing. I knew that it had to be his baby mama. I hurried and got dressed because I wanted to see what she looked like. He always made sure that I was not around when she came around. Once I was dressed, I walked in the living room but just enough so that I could hear what they were saying.

"Tez, I been blowing our phone up."

"Kam, I been busy, damn. I keep telling you that. You want a nigga to take care of you, but I gotta make money to do that. If I'm laid up, I can't," he lied; his ass ain't been doing shit. He was the same damn broke ass like he was last week. I watched as she damn near cried. That made me wonder what lies he had sold her. Tez's ass had game for days. Hell, he had my ass stuck just like he got her. He would lie through his teeth.

"You said that shit would be different but it not. I hate that I got pregnant by yo ass," she shrieked before storming off. Tez stood at the door watching her as she made her way to her car. He rubbed his hand down his face once she pulled off. I made my way back to the room. I wanted to question him on what that was about but decided to just let it go. I climbed in the bed and powered the small TV on. Each day that passed made me miss Cream and being at his house more. I was living in luxury whereas now, my ass barley had cable. This nigga's shit was always getting turned off. I laid back and thought of what I could do to get Cream back. In most people's eyes, they would say that it was too late, but in my eyes, it was never too late. I was going to get him back, even if that meant I had to kill her ass.

* * *

"Yo how much money you got? Tez ask as he walked in the bedroom. I just looked at his ass because he was getting beside his self with that bullshit. Every time I looked up he was asking for money. I don't know what was up with that shit but he was going to make this his last time.

"Tez why the fuck you always asking me for money. I don't give niggas money I keep tell you that. Now I'm going to give it to you this time but it the last time. What do you need?" I asked as I grabbed my purse. I really didn't want to pull it put in front of him because I knew that he was going to go overboard.

"I need five hundred," he told me causing me to roll my eyes. I just needed and pulled out five one hundred dollar bills and handed it to him the closed my purse. I made sure to keep it close to me because I didn't trust his ass.

He nodded and walked out the room. I waited until he left packed my shit and I headed back to my mama house. I need to put my plan in to action to get my man back. I pulled up to my mother's house and sat in the drive way for a second. My mind was all over the place. I need to think of plan. I walked in my mother's house and all the lights were out. That wasn't normal/ The living room TV was always on. I made my way to my mother room to find her and laid out in the bed sleep. I didn't want to wake her so I headed to my old room. I was happy that no one else was here because I needed to get some sleep.

15 CREAM

I was happy that Nellie was good. I knew that my brother loved her and she had become like a sister to me. Outside of that, Peaches loved her to death, and she wouldn't have been no good if Nellie would have died.

"Baby, you ready to eat?" Peaches asked as she walked in my man cave. I was looking at some files that my grandfather had sent over. The nigga Clay was connected to Nique. That made me wonder if she was in on my brother damn near being killed. I hope for her sake that she wasn't because if she was, I was going to kill her whole fucking family.

"Yes baby, I can eat. What did she cook?" I questioned. My mother loved to cook, so I knew that she threw down. She was happy anytime that she could cook. I just wanted to see how it was going to go when my grandfather got here. They had a love-hate relationship. She loved her father, but she hated the life that he lived and the life that she felt that he pulled us into. What she didn't know was that he didn't want us in the street life either—we chose to. My mom was a nurse and she felt that the money that she made was enough, but it wasn't.

We didn't live in the hood, but we went to school there. We liked having our own money and doing our own thing. Our grandfather didn't know that we were in the streets until we robbed one of his workers. He kicked our ass, put us to work, and made us work that shit off. He made us the men that we are today. I loved him for that.

I closed down my laptop before heading to the kitchen. When I walked in, my mother and Peaches were laughing and talking like they have known each other their whole lives.

"What y'all in here talking about?" I asked as I kissed Peaches.

"She was just telling me about how bad y'all was," Peaches laughed. I loved to see her smile. Just as I was replying back, my grandfather walked in the door. Soon as my mom saw that it was him, she let out a deep sigh.

"What's good Pops?" I greeted him.

"What's up son? Hey beautiful," he said, greeting my mother. He kissed her on the jaw and she gave him a fake smile. He didn't care.

"Hello father. Would you like to eat now or would you like to talk to the boys first?" my mother asked.

"Let me talk to the boys then we can all eat together. And who is this beauty?" Pops asked jokingly.

"This beauty is Tianna, but we call her Peaches. This is your future granddaughter in-law," I beamed. My Pops smiled and nodded. That me know that he approved. We headed to the room that Puff was in. Just as we were walking in, Nellie was walking out. My Pops was smiling hard. I knew that he was shocked to see Puff with someone for this long because that nigga was a straight hoe. Once we walked in the room, that nigga was laid back like he was the king of the castle.

"Nigga, she must got some good shit... yo ass got her all

75

up in here. Then you got me on a man hunt over her ass. Hell, you better marry her ass," Pops said as he took a seat on the end of the bed.

"Yes Pops, that's my baby. Hell one day, I think that I might marry her as long as she don't lie to me again," Puff told him as he sat up in the bed.

"So what the word on the streets? Puff asked.

"I got someone looking for him now, but outside of that, we have someone else to worry about. That nigga that yo mama used to fuck with, Dave, he is the nigga's uncle. So you know that they on some bullshit. I sent some niggas over there, but no one was there but the nigga's wife. I didn't have them to kill her yet. I also didn't know that the nigga was that hoe's Nique's step daddy." When my Pops said, that my mouth dropped. How didn't that shit pop up when I did the check on her? One thing that I did know was that getting to her was going to be easy.

"So what's the plan?" Pops asked. I knew that when he stepped in, then there was nothing more for us to say.

"I got some shit in motion. I just need you to keep that Nique close, just not too close. I don't want that pretty woman down there to leave you because you know I'm always looking to add to my roster," he laughed. I didn't find that shit funny. I would hate to have to hurt my Pops, but I didn't play about Peaches.

"No worries... I ain't letting that one go," I said. We talked about a few other things then we headed to the dining room so that we could have dinner. It had been a long time since my mom and grandpa had been around each other, so I was excited to see how this dinner was going to go.

"Donavan, go ahead and say grace," my mother instructed once we all were seated. I did as I was told and we all dug in. She had cooked so much food that I didn't know what to eat first. The whole room was quite I guess because we all had our heads in our plates. I was sitting across from my brother, Peaches was next to me, Nellie was next to him, and my mother was at one end of the table while my Pops was at the other end. I looked up to see my mother looking at us all smiling, that was until she noticed that my Pops was looking. That smile turned to a frown fast. I knew then that it was finna be some shit.

"Why the hell you stop smiling when you looked at me? Don't think you too old to get ya ass kicked," Pops said with a calm tone. My mom just looked; she knew better than to say anything back to him. "Matter fact, get whatever is bothering you off your chest so that we can move on because I'm old and I don't got time for this shit you be on. Now, what's up?" Pops asked. Everyone at the table looked at her, waiting on her reply. Hell, I knew that I was anyway.

"You made my boys like this. This is not how I raised them. I sent them to college to be business owners not to sell drugs. You egged them on and now, I worry every night. Daddy, I worry about you," my mom damn near cried. I kind of knew that she felt that way, but I hadn't heard her say it before. My Pops' face was priceless. I knew that it hurt him to hear her say that, but it was what it was. I felt that it needed to be said because I hated when they acted like they hated each other, well more so my mom.

"Baby girl, yo hard-headed ass sons chose this life. I didn't want it for them just like you didn't. Hell, I wanted to kill they ass when I found out. You been mad at me for all these years over nothing. I should beat you niggas asses for having my baby girl mad at me," he fussed. Me and Puff looked at each other and bussed out laughing. They got up from the table and went in the room to talk. I was happy about that because I was tired of not having family dinner like we used to when we were younger.

Once my Pops and mother were gone, I headed to my

office so that I could look over my accounts. I had an account that I had set up for Nique that I needed to move money out of. I had but half a million in there a while back. I needed to see what was left. After rolling me a blunt, I sat at my desk and pulled up the account. I damn near choked when I logged in. The account was *empty*. I had another account that was a back up account, just in case that one got low so I checked it. I started seeing red when I logged in. *"I'm going to kill this bitch!"* I said out loud. She had cleaned both accounts out—that was almost a million dollars. I pulled out my phone and dialed her number, knowing that she would answer.

"Hello," she damn near whispered.

"Bitch, when I see you, you're dead," I gritted. When I realized that she hung up, I slammed the phone down. I needed to get Scale on this shit asap. He had plenty of niggas in the streets, so I knew that he would find everyone that I was looking for.

16 NELLIE

TWO WEEKS LATER

J was so ready to get out Cream's damn house, all him and Peaches did was fuck. They got on my nerves. I mean, they didn't care where the hell they were at. I walked in on they ass in the laundry room one day. Puff was finally well enough to get out the house so we were going to his house. I was so damn happy. I wanted to walk around naked. Hell, I wanted to fuck all over the house.

"Baby, I need you to help me with my shoes," Puff said, pulling me from my thoughts. I walked over and tied them for him and then slipped mine on. Since it was late September, it was getting cool, so I had on his hoodie and some tights. He was much bigger than me so it was good and comfy. Once we had all of our stuff, we headed to the living room. Peaches was on the couch eating some chips and Cream was looking at TV. I loved them together, they were so cute.

"We finna roll," Puff told them as we headed to the door. Cream nodded and Peaches got up to hug me. Once we said our goodbyes, we headed out. He opened the door for me and I slid in, locking it soon as he closed it. I was still scared that Clay was going to come for me again. Just thinking of that made me realize that I needed to tell Puff about the real me. Amber, the church girl, loved to read and dance. I loved cooking and having fun. I just wished that I could get back to that girl. I missed my life being normal. Hell, I missed my parents, and I couldn't wait for them to meet Puff. I hoped that they loved him as much as I did. Once he was in the car, we pulled off. I couldn't help but to keep looking behind us the whole time.

"We good baby, you don't have to keep doing that," Puff said.

"I can't help it baby. I just want to make it to our destination safe," I said as he drove.

"We gone make it baby. Stop worrying," he said just as we pulled in the drive way of his house. I was so damn happy. We gathered all of our stuff then headed in the house. It smelled so damn good. Since I knew that he was going to be hungry soon, I headed straight to the kitchen. He had the housekeeper go to the store so everything I needed was already here.

I got started then headed to take a quick shower while the chicken was in the oven. When I walked in the room, he was laid back in the bed looking at ESPN. I hated that damn channel. I grabbed what I needed and headed in the bathroom. Soon as I got in, I felt a breeze so I knew that he was in the bathroom with me. The glass was steamed up so I couldn't see him. I finished cleaning myself and got out. I needed to get back in the kitchen before I burned my damn chicken up.

"Damn," I heard from behind me as I bent over to put on some socks. I stood up straight to see this damn fool standing behind me with his dick in his hands, looking like a creep.

"You are such a creep." I still hadn't told him about the

baby. I knew that I needed to but I just hadn't found the time. I was getting bigger by the day, so I knew that I was going to have to tell him soon.

"I guess that makes you an undercover hoe because you walking around with that little ass shit on showing all yo ass," he said, coming closer to me. Once he made it to me, he tugged on the shirt. I knew what that meant. I looked at the clock and saw that I had like five minutes to spare before I needed to take the chicken out. I bent over and he slid straight in. His dick was perfect for me.

"Damn baby, throw that ass back. Yo shit so wet," he moaned out. That shit was a turn on for me, and I couldn't get Clay to do that shit for nothing. He felt that talking during sex was childish. I was throwing my ass back just the way that I knew he liked it. He released his sperm in me in no time. Once we were done, I headed to get my chicken out and finished the sides.

"Baby, dinner is ready," I yelled. Shortly after, Puff came downstairs with nothing but his briefs on. I licked my lips just thinking about what I was going to do to his ass after dinner.

We sat the table and ate in silence. That was how it was most of the time. We just enjoyed being around each other. Once we finished, I cleaned up and joined him on the couch. Just as we got comfortable, his phone rung. I saw that it was his cousin Scale, so I moved so that he could get up. He walked out of the room just as he answered, so I decided to take the time to call my mother and father. I knew that they would be happy to hear from me.

"Hello," my mother's sweet voice cooed in the phone.

"Hey mommy," I smiled. I was so happy to hear her voice.

"Amber baby, how are you?" she asked, sounding as excited as I was. I knew that they missed me just as much as I missed them.

"I'm better mom. Where is dad? How is he?" I asked. They didn't know about me getting kidnapped, but they knew that I was running from Clay's crazy ass.

"He is outside working on that damn car. We were just talking about you the other day. Let me go and get him because we know that he will have a fit if he finds out you called and he didn't talk to you," she said. I could hear her moving around. I was more than sure she was in her craft room. I few moments later, I heard the door open and close.

"Baby girl," her father happily spoke. He had been calling me that for as long as I could remember.

"Hey daddy. I just wanted to hear your voice. Things are getting better and soon, I will be able to come and see y'all. I have a few friends that I want you to meet. I know you will love them. I also wanted to tell y'all that I was pregnant so y'all will be grandparents soon," I cooed. I knew that my mother was going to be happy because she loved kids. Apart of me wished that I could get them to move here. Maybe I could talk with Puff to see what we could do.

"So I'm going to be a grandfather? You mom's going to flip," he said with so much excitement. I missed them so much. I would do anything to have them here with me.

"Ok daddy, I'm going to let y'all go. I will call y'all tomorrow," I promised. I hadn't been calling much because I didn't know if Clay was fucking with them or not. He was slick and there was no telling what his ass would do. Now that he knew where I was, I knew that he wouldn't bother them.

Just as I was ending the call, Puff was walking back in the room. I could tell that he was in pain by the way that he was looking, but I learned not to say anything because that would only make him mad and I didn't have time today.

"Is everything ok?" I asked.

"Yea baby, nothing for you worry about. Who where you talking to, telling them you love them and shit?" he said with a slight attitude. I had to laugh because he knew damn well that I didn't talk to anyone but my parents and Peaches.

"I was talking to my parents baby," I told him as I scooted over so that he could get in the bed. Once he was comfortable, I kissed him and sat up. I needed to tell him about the real me because I didn't want him to think that what we have was fraud.

"Baby, it some things that I need to tell you." He looked at me like I was crazy. I knew that he thought that I was about to say something crazy by the look on his face.

"I'm listening."

"My name is Amber DeNellie Graves. I'm nineteen and my birthday is July 24. I grew up in church. My father is a pastor and my mother was a school teacher. I love dancing and cooking. I'm allergic to strawberries and I hate heights. I'm telling you this because I love you and I want to make sure that you know the real me. Nothing about me has been fake, but I avoided talking about my life because I didn't know if you knew Clay. Oh and I'm pregnant," I finished off. He just looked at me for a moment, then he sat up. I didn't know what to expect with Puff.

"So you really just going slip that in like that?"

"I mean, I needed to tell you sooo...."

"Baby, I know everything there is to know about you. You think I didn't look into you before I pursued you?" he asked. I knew that Peaches said that Cream had checked her background, but I didn't think Puff could do it on me because he didn't have my real name. I guess I was wrong.

"Look baby, I know all that I need to know. You just need to know that with me, you good. I will make sure that nothing else ever happened to you," he promised. I couldn't help but to smile. Even after everything that happened, I still feel safe with him.

"You not mad?" I asked. He looked at me like I had three heads.

"Mad for what? I knew that you was pregnant. I was just waiting on you to tell me. The doctor told me," he admitted. I just smiled. I didn't think it would be like this, but I was happy that it did.

We laid in the bed for the rest of the day, talking and making future plans. I couldn't ask for anyone else better in my life.

"*B*aby, can you go in my office and get that green folder that's on my desk?" Cream hollered from his man cave. I rolled my eyes because his office was right across the hall. I think he just wanted to get on my nerves. I hadn't been feeling well for the past few days, so he knew damn well that I didn't feel like getting up. I was on the couch looking at *Love and Hip Hop*. He knew that this was my show and that I hated to be interrupted. I got up and headed to do as he asked while it was on commercial. I grabbed the folder and headed to his man cave. When I walked in the room, he was laid back on his phone. That shit pissed me off because he was being lazy.

"Here," I said, attempting to walk off.

"Where you going?" he asked.

"Back to finish my show." I walked off before he could say something back. When I made it back in the living room, my show was coming back on. I sat back in the same spot. Just as I was fettering into the show, my phone rang. I saw that it was my mother calling so I hit ignore. I didn't have time for her shit. She had been calling me and every time I answered, she was asking me for something or saying something about me being with a nigga with money and not taking care of her. I was her daughter, not her man. That was not my job. When she hung up, I picked my phone up so that I could check my Instagram. It had been a while since I had gotten on there.

The first thing that I did was check my DM. Most of the message was from niggas, but there was a few that was from people that I didn't know. I opened one of the messages and knew that it was from Cream's ex. I had been telling him that she had been playing on my phone and he didn't believe me, but now I had proof now. I cut the TV off and headed to where he was. When I walked in, Cream had papers all over the couch. I took a seat in the chair and watched him for a second.

"Baby, what is all of this?" I asked. It looked like it was bank statements.

"Bank statements. That bitch wiped out two of my accounts. I never checked the accounts because I didn't think that I needed to. Look at this shit," he said, handing me a copy of a check. It was a check for fifty thousand dollars that she wrote to herself. I got up and looked at a few more. I didn't see how the bank didn't catch on.

"I need to get me an accountant," he stated as he lit a blunt that was on the table. I could tell that he was stressed.

"I don't have a degree, but I took a few classes before I had to stop going and take up more hours at work. I wanted to be an accountant, but I had to take care of my mama," I explained.

"Well tomorrow, you need to call and see about getting back in school. Don't worry about the money part," he told me. I couldn't contain my smile. Going to college was something that I always wanted to do.

"Oh my God baby, thank you. I will get on it first thing in

the morning," I promised him. I grabbed the papers that were all over the place and started matching them up with the checks that she wrote. This was something that I loved to do. I hoped to one day have my own firm. My mom was an accountant when I was younger. I think that's why I had a love for it. Once I was on the floor with all the papers and in my zone, I figured out how she was able to do it.

"So she had to have known someone at the bank. The same person helped her each time. She only pulled money out on Wednesday. You need to go to the bank and ask about this teller then close the accounts and open new ones," I told him before putting all of the papers up. He just nodded. I could tell that he was frustrated, so I didn't say anything else. I just got on the couch beside him. I started kissing on his neck, causing his dick to rise. I wasted no time taking care of my man. I wanted him to be stress free.

THE NEXT DAY

"*B*itch, I done broke two damn nails. Let go to the nail shop," I told Nellie. We were on FaceTime while she cooked. I didn't plan to cook at all today. I had cooked all week and I needed a break.

"Ok cool. I should be done by the time that you get here," she assured me.

"Cool. Let me go talk to his ass before I head that way," I said, ending the call. I was already dressed because I went with him to bank earlier. I finished the water that I was drinking and headed to his office. I walked in and just stood there watching his fine ass. This man was so sexy. I would have never thought that Cream would be my man.

"You being creepy and shit," he joked. I just laughed as I sat on the edge of his desk.

"So I can't look at you? I don't be saying nothing when you be doing that creepy shit. Like the other day when you was doing that shit when I got out the shower."

"I don't know what you talking about," he lied. I just shook my head because his ass knew he was lying. Cream was so much more than I thought he would be. He made me happy. I never felt this way about Tez.

"I'm finna go to the nail shop with Nellie. Are we still going to dinner tonight?"

"Yes, we can do that. Make sure that you pay attention to your surroundings."

"I will baby," I told him as I grabbed a piece of candy off his desk. Since Clay was still on the loose, he had been talking me anywhere I needed to go. This was the first time that I was going somewhere without him. I knew that he was going to have someone follow us because he was so overprotective. Hell, he was letting me off easy. I was more than sure that Puff was not going to let Nellie off that easy. Cream's phone rang and he answered, putting it on speaker.

"Aye nigga, where Peaches at? Who in the hell told them that they was going somewhere? Y'all better pay a motherfucker to come and do all nails because y'all not going no damn where. It too much going on, and I just can't take any chances so tell Peaches' ass you can cancel that shit. They only way y'all going to the nail shop is if one of us take y'all, and I know I'm not going to no damn nail shop," Puff fussed. I couldn't do shit but laugh.

"Well, I guess you not going to the nail shop," Cream laughed. I didn't find that shit funny. I was ready to live my life and not have to look over my shoulder. I flopped down in the chair that was on the side of his desk.

"Stop looking like that baby... this shit will all be over soon. We just waiting for Puff to get better," he told me before kissing me. Since going to the nail shop was out, I grabbed my phone so I could find someone to come to me. I knew there was plenty of people on Instagram. The problem was that Cream was picky, so I would have to find someone that he approves and get a background check on. So I know that will take another day. I wanted to pop all these damn nails off.

18 PUFF

I knew that Peaches and Nellie were mad because I shut that nail shit down, but I was not finna let shit happen to them, just so they can get the fucking nails done. The Clay nigga seemed to have disappeared and so had Nique. I walked in the living room and Nellie was sitting on the couch looking sad like that was going change what the fuck I said. She could be mad all she wanted, but I was protecting her and she needed to understand that. I walked to the back yard so that I could smoke and calm my nerves. I had been getting calls all morning from Lipz; she had been on some other shit that I didn't have time for. That bitch was gone make me kill her ass.

I looked down to see that my phone was ringing once again. "Why you keep calling my phone?" I asked her soon as I answered. I still owe her for that shit that she did at the hospital.

"Puff, I miss you. Why you haven't been calling me? Why didn't you tell me that you were still alive?" she asked as if she didn't know that I didn't fuck with her and furthermore, that I had a woman.

"Yo, I don't fuck with you like that, so why the fuck would I tell you my business? Stop calling me hoe," I said before hanging up. I blocked her ass because I didn't need her ass calling and my baby answered or saw her calling at all.

We needed to get this Clay nigga sooner than later. My baby was ready to live her life. I pulled out my phone and called my brother. "I'm finna bring Nellie over, we need to hit the streets and find this nigga. I just sent Pops' tech a email. I needed to know everybody that nigga know. I'm going to find his ass. We do this shit for a living, so there is no way that we shouldn't be able to find his ass," I told Cream as I made my way back in the house. We talked a while longer before I went to find her mean ass. This baby was making her a brat. But she was *my* brat so I was all for it. I walked around the house until I found her in my office looking at TV. I had no idea why she like coming it here. There was a million other places that she could watch TV in this house, but she always end up in here.

"Go put some clothes on baby," I advised before sitting at my desk. She just got up and walked out the room. I took that time to do some research of my own. Soon as she was ready, we headed out the door. I felt bad on the ride to Cream's house because she was consistently looking behind us. That shit fucked my baby up and I was going to fuck him up for her.

"Baby, can I ask a favor?" she said, pulling me from my thoughts.

"What's good baby?"

"When you find Clay, can I be the one to kill him? I have been dreaming about killing him for a long time. I feel like it will make me feel better. I hate fearing for my life. I hate being scared to ride in a car. Most nights, I don't sleep because I feel like he is coming to find me. I don't want to live like this," she cried. I didn't know if she was really crying or if it was the baby, but I wasn't with that shit.

"I would call that a favor, but I will see what I can do baby," I promised. We pulled up at Cream's house just as Scale did. I helped my baby out the car and we made our way in the house. While I waited for Cream to shower, I called my cousin Mia. I needed to do something to make my baby happy.

"What's good cuz?" she asked when she answered.

"Yo gal still do nails and shit?"

"Yea, she just got her own shop. What's up?" Mia was the finest nigga look bitch I knew. Back in the day, we used to pull bitches together. When they made that gay marriage shit legal, she settled down.

"Can you have her come over to Cream's spot? I need her to take care of my girl and Cream's girl nails. With all the shit going on, I don't need them out without us cause ain't no way I'm going in no damn nail shop. Plus, we niggas be on the streets looking for this nigga," I told her.

"Aite nigga, we're finna head that way. Don't leave without me nigga. It been a minute since I put some work in. She be having a nigga stuck under her ass," Mia admitted. I couldn't do shit but laugh because I knew that I was going to be the same way. I went in the living room where Nellie and Peaches were and sat in-between them. There really wasn't any room, but I made some. They both was looking all ugly and frowned up.

"Tell me y'all love me?" I said as I wrapped my arms around the both of them.

"But we don't right now," Peaches said, causing me to do a double take.

"Damn, my feelings hurt... you don't love my brother either? I thought I could away depend on my sister to love me... guess I will tell the nail lady that I have coming that y'all don't need her," I said, acting as if I was pulling my phone out to call someone. Nellie snatched it out my hand fast as hell. I couldn't do shit but laugh. We sat on the couch and looked at what I called ratchet TV. Them hoes talked too much and acted out every chance they got. If Nellie did that shit, I would kick her ass. Now it would be different if someone started with her.

The doorbell rang and Peaches picked her phone up. I knew that she was looking to see who it was. If they made it in the gate, then it had to be someone that was invited, so I knew that it was Mia. I went to open the door for her. Soon as they came in, her girl got right to work. Cream's slow ass finally came down the stairs. That nigga always took forever. We smoked a blunt then headed out. The first place that I was going was to Nique's mom again.

"Pops called while I was in my room. He sent a few addresses that he said that we needed to check. Also, he said to find that nigga's uncle and we will find him."

"That nigga probably on the track," Mia said. I had updated her on what all was going on while we waited on Cream's slow ass. I jumped on the e-way and headed that way. The nigga's uncle called himself a pimp, but all he really did was turn crackheads into hoes. The only normal female that I ever heard of him fucking with was Nique's mama. It took us a while to get to the track since it was in the hood. When we made it, Dave wasn't hard to fine. I pulled out on the neighborhood crackhead name Ms. Janice and she pointed me straight to his ass. She hated that nigga because he tried to kill her a few years back. I fucked with Ms. Janice; she was real as hell and did her own thing. We pulled over and watched him for a while. I wanted to catch his ass slipping, but one thing for sure, his ass was going to be dead soon.

19 CREAM

I couldn't wait for this shit to be over. I had so much shit in the works that I didn't need this beef fucking it up. I hadn't told my brother yet, but I was getting shit set up for us to purchase another hotel. I was trying to get us out of this street shit. I just wanted to run this shit from the background. I was over this street shit. I wanted to enjoy the fruits of my labor. I wanted to travel the world with my girl and baby. If I could land this deal, we would have Scale and Dre running this shit for us. I made a mental note to have a meeting with him and Dre. In the past few weeks, Dre has shown his loyalty to us.

"That nigga getting in his car. Let follow his ass," Mia recommended. I was so into my thoughts that I wasn't paying attention at all. I was glad to know that they were. Puff pulled off as soon as Dave did but made sure to stay a little behind so that he wouldn't see us. When Dave pulled up to the house that we found Nellie at, I knew that we had hit the jackpot. We parked across the street. It was crazy how he didn't notice us. He was too busy trying to get in the house. I called Scale because I needed have them on standby. I was going to kill all of them at one time. We waited a few minute just to make sure that no one else was coming before we got out.

"Ok, I have Scale on the way with the van. We gone grab this nigga and take him to the warehouse. I want to kill all of they asses at once," I told them as we walked up to the door. Soon as we walked up, Puff kicked the door down. This nasty ass nigga was hitting a crackhead from the back. When Dave turned around, he hurried and pulled his pants up.

"You a nasty motherfucker," Puff said, grabbing his ass. The crackhead thought that she was going to get away, but I grabbed her ass before she had a chance. This was one of them situation where she was in the wrong place at the wrong time. We tied them both up and waited for Scale. Once we had him in the van, we killed the female and threw her ass right in the truck with him.

"The next stop is Nique's mama spot," Puff said as we headed that way. When we pulled up, Nique's car was in the driveway. I smiled because I was finally going to get her ass. We parked in front of the house that was next to hers.

"Mia, you got to the front… we gone go to the back. If she see us, she's gone panic," I said as we walked up. I stood to the side when she knocked on the door. Soon as it opened, Mia pushed her way in and we went in right behind her.

"Damn baby, I been calling you," I said, grabbing Nique by her hair. That bitch thought that she was going to run.

"Cream," she cried. Her mama was laid out on the couch beat up. I was guessing that Dave had beaten her ass. If her daughter didn't fuck me over the way that she did, I may have thought about letting her live.

"So you ready to tell me where that nigga at and where my money at?" I gritted. I didn't come to play with her ass.

Nique was crying so hard that she couldn't talk. "You got two seconds."

"I don't know... he left earlier," she managed to get out. I didn't want to hear that shit. Mia grabbed Nique's phone off the floor and handed it to her.

"Call that nigga and tell him that he need to get here quick," Mia told her with her gun to her head. Nique's hands were shaking so bad that she could barely dial the nigga's number.

"Baby, please get here now," she cried soon as Clay answered. I knew that he was going to come running and that was just what I wanted. We cut all the lights out except the one that was in the hallway, so he that he wouldn't see who was in the house. They had a big ass window in the dining room, and when you pulled on the street, you could see straight in. It took him no more than five minutes to pull up. I knew that was going to be quick because Scale was already outside waiting.

Puff stood next to the door, waiting on him to come in. Soon as he did, Puff's gun went up. Clay felt the barrel before he realized what was going on. "Bitch, you set me up!" was the first thing that he said. He could see who all was in the room, so I did him a favor and cut the lights on. When he laid his eyes on Puff, Clay looked like he could have shitted on himself.

"So first thing first, where in the fuck is my money?" Puff asked.

"That bitch you fucking stole it," he lied. Puff looked at his ass like he was crazy. "Yea Amber stole it, that's why I came looking for her in the first place," he admitted. Scale walked in a few seconds later with some rope and tape.

"Get this nigga and his bitch out of here?!" I said before walking out the house. Lucky for us, it was dark so no one would know what was going on. Once they had all of them in the van, we all headed to the warehouse. When we pulled up, Puff jumped in his car and said that he would be back and not to do anything until he returned. So while we waited, I booked me and my baby a trip to Mexico. With all the shit that had been going on, we needed a break.

20 NELLIE

"$\mathcal{I}$'m so happy that we will be having our babies together. They are going to grow up and be best friend just like we are," I said as I stuck a scoop of ice cream in my mouth. We were waiting on Puff and Cream to get back so that we could go to dinner. They didn't know that we were going but that would when they walked through that door. They had been gone a while. Puff wouldn't tell me what they went to do, and I really didn't care as long as he made it back to me. That was my only concern.

"Bitch, don't neither one of us knows what we having... besides, they will be cousin anyway so they will close," she shrugged. She was right. I didn't think about that.

"Peaches, you just don't know how happy I am that we met each other. I don't know where I would be right now. Hell, I would probably be somewhere dead," I told her. I knew that my life was a mess before coming here. Clay was going to kill me the way that he had been kicking my ass. That nigga beat my ass if I fixed him a glass of ice water and it didn't have enough cubes. I remember the first time he beat my ass like it was yesterday.

"Baby, I'm finna go to the church with my mama," I yelled from downstairs. We had just moved in our house. He was good to me that my ass was head over hills for his ass. Just as I was walking towards the door, he called my name. I turned around and he was on his phone smiling at something. I wanted to knock that damn phone out his hand, but I didn't. I just asked who he was talking to. Soon as the words left my mouth, he slapped my ass so hard that my mouth started bleeding. I was shocked that I didn't know what to do. I just stood there.

"Don't ever fucking question me!" he said before walking off. I couldn't believe he had hit me. From that point, I was getting my ass beat. In the begging it wasn't as bad but after he realized that I was just letting him do whatever he wanted he took advantage of that. He ruined me. It had taken time but I was a much stronger person because of what he took me through. I hate that I went through it but I wouldn't change it. It made me the woman I am today.

"Don't say that boo. God wasn't ready for you to leave. He brought you through it so that's all that matters. Just know that you will have a sister in me for the rest of your life," she said, interrupting my moment down memory lane. I don't know if it was the baby or what but my ass was crying so damn hard. Just as I broke down, Puff rushed in the door. I could look in his face and tell that something was wrong.

"Y'all come on, we gotta go," he said, causing us both to jump up. I slipped my shoes on and Peaches went to change. She had on some little ass shorts and she knew better than to walk out like that or Cream would kill her ass. Once she came down the stairs, we headed to the car. The whole ride to wherever we were going was quite. I don't know what was on their minds, but I was thinking about my mama's famous peach cobbler. I couldn't wait to taste it. This baby had me wanting the craziest shit. The other day, I woke Puff up and had him to go and get me a pickle and some mayo in the squeeze bottle. That shit was so damn good. Puff was pissed but I didn't care; he knew that I wanted what I wanted.

We pulled up to what looked like a office building but went straight to the back. Soon as we turned the corner, a door lifted. He helped us both out the car before walking off. I looked at Peaches and she just shrugged. Her ass was getting big. If I just knew that her ass was going to have twins. She hated to hear it but it was the truth. We followed him until we came to a room that was closed off. You could see that people where in there, but the glass was frosted so it was hard to see what was going on.

"What the hell?" Peaches called out when we walked in. There was people tied up in the chairs, but we couldn't see their faces because they had bags on them. I could tell that it was two men and two women because of their shoes. I walked over to the tabled because I wanted to sit down. My ass was lazy.

I looked at Puff and he nodded to the guy that was standing on the other side of the room. He pulled the bags from over their heads one by one. I was shocked to say the least.

"Amber, baby, tell them that you took the money," Clay said as soon as they took the bag off his head. I just looked at his ass.

"Clay, it doesn't matter. You think that he would get mad at me? The money is gone, so what do you want me to say?" I shrugged.

"See I told y'all that she had the money. Now y'all can let me go," Clay said, causing us all to laugh. He thought that it was going to be that easy. I leaned back in the chair and rubbed my stomach. When I did that, Clay's eyes damn near popped out of his head. I had an oversize shirt on, so when I walked in, you really couldn't see how big my stomach was.

"You let that nigga get you pregnant?" his dumb ass asked.

"Naw, I swallowed a fucking ball, what do you think?" I said as I propped my feet up. Clay tried to jump up but he was chained to the chair.

"Shit, that pussy so good I couldn't pull out," Puff said as he kissed me. Clay was doing his best to get out of the chair. What he didn't realize was that he was hurting himself because there was no getting up for him.

"Y'all so nasty," Peaches said as she sat on the other said of the table.

"Fuckk all that! You ready to tell me where my money at?" Cream said as he made his way over to Nique. Her mother was right next to her and she looked like she was scared for her life. Nique looked to whom I assumed was her stepfather. He was just still, looking like a bump on a log. His face didn't hold an expression. It was as if he was unbothered.

"What you looking at his ass for? He can't save you," Cream told her as he took as seat next to Peaches.

"Amber, baby, look… I'm sorry for everything," Clay said, causing us all to look his way. I just busted out laughing because I knew that he couldn't be serious. I stood up and made my way to him.

"Clay, there's isn't enough 'I'm sorry' in the world to make me forgive you," I said, walking off towards Puff. I grabbed his gun from his hand and sent a bullet through Clay's head, causing it to explode like a watermelon. I stood there for a second and then turned around and handed Puff his gun back. Everyone in the room was looking at me like I was crazy.

"Why y'all looking at me like that? I been waiting years to do that," I said, sitting back down in the same chair.

"I'm trying to see when the fuck you learned to shoot like that," Puff said. "Aye, my dad taught me. When I was young, he took me to the range all the time," I shrugged. I had been shooting guns since I was ten. My dad loved guns, so we always went to gun shows and shit like that. I've owned a gun since I was sixteen.

21 PEACHES

$\mathcal{I}$ sat back and watched Cream question Nique. It was beyond me why he was even doing all of that because she wasn't going to give him the answers that he wanted. It had been an hour since Nellie blew Clay's head off and looking at his body straddling the chair was making me sick to the stomach, that or my baby was ready for me to eat. No matter which it was, leaving here was the answer to my problems.

"Can you kill this bitch already? I'm hungry and I'm tired of looking at that," I said, pointing to Clay's body. Cream just looked at me.

"I wish I would have just killed yo ass the day that I damn near ran yo ass over," Nique said, causing me to look at her.

"Aw so that *was* you?" I asked for clarification.

"Cream, baby, look… we can make us work. She don't love you. That bitch been still fucking her ex. I think that's his baby, at least that's what he told me," Nique lied. I looked to Cream. He had the look of disappointment on his face. He had to know that she was playing mind games. He had to.

The other guy that I found out was named Dave busted out laughing.

"What the fuck you laughing at?" I asked. This guy was the same one that damn near killed my mother years ago. I would never forget his face.

"I didn't take you for the type that didn't know who her baby daddy is. You seem like a good girl, but I guess that's just a look. I guess you a hoe like yo mama," he shrugged. I picked up the bat that was on the table and hit him across his knees, causing him to cry out in pain. I owed his ass for what he did to my mama.

"Shut the fuck up!" I hollered. I didn't even know that I could hit that damn hard, but it was good to know. Nique's mom started crying loud as hell and it was getting on my nerves, so I hit her ass across the head. She had been crying since we fucking walked in. All that shit for nothing her ass was going to leave the same way that all of them were.

"Bitch, you better be glad that I'm chained to this chair or I would beat yo ass," Nique fumed.

"Bitch, even if you wasn't chained, you wouldn't do shit. You a weak bitch. You had more than enough chance to beat my ass and you did nothing," I said, going to sit down. I was tired that damn fast. My ass was almost six months pregnant so all of that moving was getting to me. Nique thought that she was doing something by telling Cream that but she wasn't. He knew that I would never fuck with that nigga again. Tez had gotten my fucking best friend pregnant. That nigga couldn't even get a conversation out of my ass.

"I'm hungry," Nellie said before getting up and taking Cream's gun. She sent a bullet through each of their heads before handing the gun back to him. "Now can we go and get something to eat?"

I was in shock because this wasn't the Nellie that I knew.

She was so timid and laid back. Seeing her like this was new for me. I mean, she took all of their lives without a second thought. Just as she was walking towards the door, Scale walked in.

"Damn, I missed the fun?" he quizzed. Nellie's ass just kept walking. Puff just followed behind her. Once they were gone, I watched as they disposed of the bodies. Cream was ready to go, but I wanted to watch for some reason. I was fascinated at what they were doing.

"You like this shit?" Cream asked.

"Yea. I wanted to be there when y'all did it at the hotel. I snuck up there but y'all got done so fast. I know you think that I was downstairs but I wasn't. I had the cordless phone." He just laughed. That was the first time he smiled since Nique said that shit about me fucking Tez. I wanted to ask Cream did he believe her, but I didn't feel that it was worth talking about. I didn't want his ass... periodt.

An hour later, we were headed out the door. I was hungry as hell. "Baby, what you want to eat?" Cream asked.

"I want some Waffle House with a side of you and that good dick," I said as I walked out in front of him.

"Your nasty ass always ready to fuck."

"Nigga, we don't fuck... we make love," I joked as he closed the car door. When he got in, Cream looked me then pulled me in for a kiss.

"How about we have the chef to come over and make us breakfast? You can get this dick while we wait," he smiled. I nodded and laid back since I knew that we had a while before we got to the house. For some reason, I kept thinking about my mother. I pulled my phone out and called her, but I didn't get any answer. It was cool because I was going to go and check on her. I just prayed that she would be ready to get some help. I missed the old her and wanted her back in my life. I wanted my baby to know their grandmother.

* * *

"Baby, I'm finna go get Nellie and then go and check on my mother," I hollered to Cream. He was in his office as always. He was opening a new building so he had been busy with that. I had been planning to go and check on my mom for a while, but I hadn't been feeling well. It had been almost three weeks since Nellie had killed Clay them. It was so crazy that it didn't bother her at all. It was like it hadn't happened.

"Ok, I'm headed out. Don't forget that we have an appointment today at four," Cream said as he came into the living room. I don't know what made him think that I was going to forget about my appointment to find out what I was having. We had been pushing it off because everyone wanted to be there. I had to find a time that was good for everyone. Nellie was a few weeks behind me, so she was going find out today as well. It was my day, so there was no way that I was going to forget. I just walked off.

"No kiss?" he said, smoking behind me. I turned around with the biggest smile on my face. I kissed my baby and headed out. I jumped in my Porsche truck and headed to get Nellie's ass. I pulled up to Pops' house since they were still there until their house got finished. I knew that Pops was going to come outside because he always did. He was the grandfather that I didn't have. He always looked out for us.

"Hey baby girl," he greeted me as soon as I got out the truck.

"Hey Pops," I greeted him back. When I walked in, Nellie was getting ready to walk out. I just turned around and strolled back to my truck. Pops made sure that we were in the truck good before we pulled off. Neither of us talked for a moment. The only sound in the car was Ella Mai. I was thinking about the past year of my life. It had almost been a year since me and Cream met. Who would have thought that shit would be like this? I was so in love and I knew that he felt the same way, unlike Tez.

"Have you tried calling her again?" Nellie questioned. I had been calling my mother for the past few weeks and hadn't gotten an answer. I found out that she was still in the apartment because I called the manager, and he told me that she had been paying her rent.

"Naw girl. My ass done called a million times. I gave up on calling," I explained. She was not answering at all. I had no idea what was going on, but I was about to find out today. We made small talk until we turned on her street. I parked then we both got out.

"Damn Peaches, yo ass done let Tez knock you up too?" Marcus asked as soon as he laid eyes on me.

"Hell no! I would never," I said, walking up to my mother's door. I didn't want talk to his ass. I didn't know who the hell Cream had watching me, and I didn't need to hear his mouth. I walked in the door and as always, it was a mess.

"Ma," I called out. I walked through the house to see if I could find her. I went from room to room. It wasn't that big but my ass was big, so it took some time. I didn't see her in her room, so I went to my old room. She wasn't there either. I knew damn well she didn't leave with the house opened because her TV and stuff was still here.

"Peaches," I heard Nellie call out. I rushed to see where she was because there was panic in her voice. I found her in my old bathroom. My mother was laid out on the floor. I could tell that she had OD'd. I pulled out my phone and called 911. Nellie helped me drag her to the shower and we prayed that would help. Once the paramedics was here, I called Cream and told him what was going on. We jumped in the truck and followed the ambulance to the hospital. Soon as we pulled up, so did Cream and Puff. I was a wreck. I prayed the whole way here that my mother would be ok. I needed her to be ok. She was all that I had outside of Cream them.

22 CREAM

"What's going on baby?" I questioned when I walked in the ER. Peaches looked like she had been crying. I was trying to ask her on the phone what was going on, but she couldn't really say. She just said that it was something with her mother. I hadn't really heard her talking about her mother much, so I didn't know anything about her. All I knew was that she was on drugs. I figured when Peaches was ready to talk, she would tell me. When she told me that she was going to check on her mom, I didn't think anything of it. I felt if it was something bad, she would have told me. She always had good things to say about her mother, so I was thinking that her mother was just going through a phase.

"She was laying there and stuff was coming out her mouth," Peaches explained through tears. That mean that she had an overdose. I just hoped they got to her in time because if not, she wasn't going to make it. We sat in the lobby for hours waiting to hear something. Peaches had been to the desk so many damn times that I was sure that they were tired of seeing her.

"Family of Janice Jenkins," a doctor walked from the back

and called out. Peaches jumped up and walked over to him. I followed behind. I didn't know what kind of news she was about to get, so I wanted to make sure that I was right there with her.

"I'm her daughter."

"Janice overdosed as you know. We had to pump her stomach. She's going to be ok but she needs help," he explained. Afterwards, he ushered us to the room that she was in. I was shocked to see that Ms. Janice was her mother. If I would have known that, I would have made niggas stop serving her along tome ago.

"Ma," Peaches cried as she made her way to her mother's side. She looked so weak. I felt bad for the both of them. Ms. Janice had a shock expression on her face as she watched Peaches make her way over to her. That let me know that she didn't know that Peaches was pregnant.

"I'm so happy that you are ok ma. I was so scared," she told her. Soon as she made it to her mother, she put her hand on Peaches' stomach. "Yes, I'm having a baby. We are going to find out what we are having in few hours. Ma, I need you to get better so that you can be here to see you grandbaby grow up."

Her mother just smiled. She looked up and saw me. "Nigga, you done knocked my baby up?" Ms. Janice said, causing me to laugh. I guess she was good because she wasn't having problem talking shit as always.

"I'm going to marry her too so it's cool," I said as I pulled Peaches close to me. I looked at the time and saw that we only had a hour till it was time for us to go to the doctor. I guess Peaches noticed to because she told her mom that we would come by later and bring her something to eat.

On the way to the car, I called Pops to let him know that we were on the way. I was more than sure that his old ass was early. Nellie and Puff were already gone. Luckily, the doctor's office wasn't far. We made it there just in time. Pops had already signed us in so we were just waiting.

"I hope it some girls cause y'all niggas getting on my nerves," Pops said, making the whole waiting room laugh. That old man was something else, but I would want anyone else to be my grandfather.

They called us to the back at the same time. I would have never thought that me and my brother would be having a baby at the same time. Hell, I didn't think that I would ever have any kids. For a long time, I didn't want kids. I knew the streets. I had been waiting to get out for a while, but now, I had the motivation that I needed. I was going to be done with this street shit. I wanted to be able to see my baby grow up. I didn't want to be one of them daddies that just bought their kids shit. I wanted to be there for everything.

"Ok let see," the doctor said as me and Puff helped them on the table. Nellie was going first since she was the closet to the doctor. The doctor put some jelly shit on her and cut the machine on. The sound of the baby's heart beat was so loud. That shit had my brother smiling big as hell. I was happy for him. He had found someone to break that wall that he had up. "Looks like there's a lil princess baking."

If I didn't know any better, I would have thought that that nigga was about to cry. "Thank God! Let's just pray that they both girls because I swear we don't need no mo niggas in this family," Pops said, making us all laugh once again. The doctor printed a few pictures for them before making her way to Peaches. I could tell that she was nervous but I didn't see why. I didn't care what we had as long as it was healthy. I would love to have a son, but I wouldn't trip if it was a girl.

"Ummm..." the doctor said as she moved the thing around on Peaches' stomach. The whole room was quiet as she did her thing. "Look... there is two. One is a girl and the other is a...... boy," she told us. Peaches' ass bussed out crying, and it wasn't a happy cry either. It took everything not laugh. Especially since my damn brother was cracking up.

"Look again," she cried. The doctor looked like she wanted to laugh too, but I was sure that she knew better. She did as she was told and got the same result. Peaches sat up and wiped the gel off of her. Pops was just looking because I was more than sure that he hadn't ever seen her act like that. I had to force her ass to get back on the table so that the lady could give us some pictures. Peaches didn't talk at all on the way back to the hospital to check in on her mom. I couldn't wait till her attitude was gone so that I could made fun of her. We all had been telling her that she was having twins, but she didn't want to listen. I bet she will next time.

23 TEZ

"Damn nigga, yo bitch done disappeared on you?" Raye said as I drove to Nique's mama house. I had been calling her for the past few weeks and she hadn't been answering. I was getting low on money and needed her to give me some. Nique really wasn't a bad female—she was just dumb. She was too hard up for a nigga. As long as niggas fucked her good, she was going to do whatever. That's part of the reason that I didn't fuck with her like that. The thing that made me fuck with her was the fact that she was fucking with that Cream nigga. That nigga was paid and I wanted what he had. She was going to be my way to it. I pulled to her mother's house and knocked on the door. No one came to the door. I walked back to the car and called her ass again. I knew that Raye was going to have something to say. That nigga was on me about getting her to talk when he was the right hand to their right hand. All he had to do was stop being a snake and keep the Scale nigga close. Word on the street was that they were passing shit on to him. This nigga was so damn dumb.

"Fuck that bitch!" I expressed. I was pissed. We headed

back to my mother's house so that I could think about what I wanted to do. The whole ride there, I listened to Raye talk to his baby mama on the phone. They seemed to be talking 'bout everything but nothing. I started to tune him out until he told her to hold on because Scale was calling. Raye acted like he was scared of that nigga. I would have robbed his ass blind a long time ago. He could do that shit with ease.

"I haven't been to the trap today... I been taking care of some other shit. I'm finna head that way in a minute. What's up?" It was hard for me to really hear what Scale was saying so I cut the radio down. His phone was normally loud as hell, but I guess Raye cut it down. "I did do the count and it was short when that nigga brought it there...... aight, I'm headed that way," was the last thing he said before ending the call.

"What was that about?" I quizzed being nosey.

"That money that I grabbed for yo ass."

I could see the fear in that nigga's eyes. I needed him to man the fuck up. "Damn, you gone let that nigga scare you? Them nigga having plenty of money... that little shit ain't nothing. You that nigga's right hand and should be getting just as much money as he's getting, but he got you out here damn near struggling. Besides, Cream dem look at his ass when shit's not right. I would get enough money from they ass to start my own shit. I know you don't want to work yo ass off forever. We both know that even if they handed shit over to him, they going to make sure that they still be running it. You and Scale been rocking it for a long time and that nigga is not taking you to the top with him. If you think that shit, you a fool. That nigga already be with that lil nigga Dre all the time. Now tell me that anything I just said was a lie," I said to convince him more. I needed him on board because Scale was our way to the money now that Nique's ass had disappeared. Raye just sat there like he was thinking about what I had said.

"Let me think about it." I pulled to the corner down the street from the trap because Scale didn't want the nigga hanging with me. Raye told me a while back that Scale said I was a snake because I got my girl's best friend pregnant. That was bullshit though. Kam wasn't really Peaches' best friend because if she was, she wouldn't have fucked me. I didn't make her ass to do that shit. She did it because that's what she wanted to do. Thinking of Kam, I needed to stop by her house. She didn't live far from where I dropped Raye off at so it took me no time to get there.

I saw that her mom was home, so I called Kam to see how long she was going to be there. Her mom hated my ass but I didn't care.

"How long yo mama finna be there? I thought you said that she had to work today?" I questioned. I could tell that I was pissing her off but I didn't care.

"Damn, she finna get ready to go Tez. You calling and questioning me like you pay bills here or something."

"I didn't say all that... I just asked a question, damn. You tripping," I told her before hanging up. I would just come back later because she was on some other shit. I headed back to my mom's house so that I could see what she had up. I was in her car so I wanted to make sure she didn't needed to go anywhere. I had my own car but hers was better, so I always drove it. I pulled up at home and my mom was on the porch talking on the phone as always.

"Hey ma."

"Hey baby. I need you to go to the store for me. The list and the money on the table,' she informed me as I walked into her house. I grabbed the list and money then headed to the bathroom before going back out the door. Walmart was the closest store so I headed there. On the ride there, I kept thinking about Peaches. I missed her. I knew that after I robbed Cream, she was going to come running back to me and I was going to accept her with open arms. She was only with that nigga because he had money. Soon as I get her, I'm going to put a baby in her ass.

I pulled on Walmart lot and headed in. I hated this damn store because there was always a million people here. I grabbed a basket and headed to get the shit that was on this list. My mama always needed some shit. As I headed to the aisle where the cleaning stuff was, I saw a girl that looked like Peaches. I grabbed what I needed and headed in the direction that the girl walked in. It had been a while since I last saw Peaches, so it may not have been her, but I was going to check and be sure. Soon as I got closer, I heard her talking to someone on the phone and knew that it was her. Her back was facing me, so I walked up and tapped her on the shoulder. When she turned around, I got the shock of my life.

"Yo, please tell me that you just fat and you didn't let that nigga knock you up?" I asked even though I knew the answer to the question that I was asking. I couldn't believe that she would do some shit like that to me. Peaches knew that I wanted her back and she let that nigga fuck raw.

"Tez, why are you talking to me?" she asked me as if I was really doing something wrong. She was mine no matter who she was fucking with, so what did she mean why was I talking to her? Peaches attempted to walk off, but I grabbed her arm, pulling her back to me.

"Don't fucking walk off from me." She looked down at my hand like I was a junkie on the street and I touched her. It was like she had turned into someone else. The Peaches that I knew wouldn't have done nothing like that.

"I would advise you get yo hand off me," she gritted. I mean, Peaches sounded like she ready meant the shit. Peaches was never the type to talk back, so I guess the nigga had given her some back bone. Just as I was about to say something, some big ass nigga walked over.

"It there a problem Mrs. Latham?" he asked her.

"No Bones, he was just leaving," she said with a smile. I just nodded and walked off. He had called her by that nigga's last name, which meant that she had married his ass. I was for sure going to kill his ass now. I got the rest of the stuff that my mom needed and hurried out the store. I sat in my car until I saw her come out. I couldn't believe my eyes when I saw her getting in to a white Bentley. I pulled out my phone and called Raye. I knew just how we were going to get they ass.

24 SCALE

*R*aye had to be the dumbest nigga that I knew. I couldn't believe that we had been friends this long and nothing about me rubbed off on him. I knew that he was the one that had stolen the money. See, what he didn't know was that before Dre dropped the money off, I had already did the count and so had Dre. When Dre first pointed it out, I didn't want to believe that Raye would cross me like that. It took for Dre to show me. Raye was next in line, all he had to do was stay loyal. I knew that Cream and Puff where stepping down and shit was going to be handed over to me. See Raye was a spender. He didn't know how to save money. He cared more about showing off than he did anything.

I had him come to the trap so that I could count the money in front of him. I really didn't want to get Cream and Puff involved, but it looked like that's what I was going to have to do. I was sitting in the back room looking at Raye on the cameras that he didn't know was here. I had covered for his ass for too long. I couldn't tell you how much money I had added so that his ass wouldn't get killed. I was done doing that shit. I had a family that I had to take care of. He didn't care so neither did I at this point. I got my shit ready and headed out. I needed to go pick up my nagging ass baby mama.

"Aye I'm ok, but I need you to stay here and get this money till I get back," I told Raye as I made my way to my car. I had just copped me a new BMW. I had been wanting this car for a while. When they promoted me, it was the first thing that I got myself.

"Aite," was all Raye said before going back to his conversation. I pulled off then called Cream. I needed to let him know what was up. I hated to do it because I knew that he was going to say he told me so. I just wanted to give Raye ass the benefit of the doubt because he was my nigga. My mom and his mom used to be best friends. I knew that it was going to hurt his mom but her son was a snake.

"What's good nigga?" Cream answered.

"Shit really. I got some shit to handle with Alisha then I will be going back to the trap. When I get back, I'ma need y'all to come by. It some shit we need to handle," I explained. As always, he didn't ask any questions; he just said to call him when it was time. An hour later, I was picking her up. She worked at a call center and had been there for a year now. She gave birth to my son SJ a year ago. My son was the reason that I grinned that way that I did. I didn't want him to have to do the shit that I was doing to get by.

"Hey baby," she said, getting in the car. I made a mental note to get her ass a car because I was tired of picking her up.

"Hey you hungry?" I asked. I remembered this morning that she forgotten her lunch so more than likely, she hadn't eaten anything.

"Nah, I'm good. I'm going to cook dinner tonight so I can wait," she told me. I just nodded because Alisha always said that she was going to cook and then her hoe ass friend would come around and all that would change. The thing that I hated about Alisha was that she wanted to live like she was single.

I dropped her off at the house and headed back to the trap. When I got there, Dre was in the living room playing the game. I made my way to the back of the house. Raye was in the room on the phone. I was going to buss in but decided to just listen for a second.

"Naw, I told yo ass he's not here. Nobody's here but Dre, so it would be the perfect time. We can pin the shit on him. The room locked ...... I know for a fact that's where the money at....... Aye, let me check shit out... be here in thirty minutes."

When he hung up, I walked back to the front and told Dre not to tell him I came. I went to the car and called Cream and Puff. I needed them to be here. I moved my car down the street so that he wouldn't see it. I told them to do the same. I waited in my car till they pulled up. I texted Raye and told him that I was going to be gone for a while. They got in with me and we watched the house to see who was going to pull up. I texted Dre and let him know what was finna go down. I fucked with Dre. He was loyal and about his money.

"I told him to keep that nigga away from here," I said when I saw the Tez nigga pulling up. "I just know that he was not talking to that soft ass nigga. That's the nigga that yo girl used to fuck with," I told Cream. He was in the back seat, so he leaned up so that he could get a better look. We got out after that. When we walked up to the door, Raye had a gun to Dre's head and Tez was in the back of the house.

"Damn, that's how we doing shit?" I said, scaring the hell out of him. Raye was so into talking shit to Dre that he didn't hear us come in the door.

"This nigga was stealing," he lied. We all bussed out laughing, including Dre. This nigga thought that we were dumb.

Cream walked to the back. Puff closed the door and leaned against the wall.

"So if that's the case, what this nigga was doing? Because it looks to me like y'all was trying to rob me," Cream said as he walked in the room with his gun to Tez's head. Raye opened his mouth to lie and I emptied my clip in his ass. I was over this nigga trying to play me. Puff was still at the door. Just as Tez was getting ready to talk, Puff sent one shot through that nigga's head. His brain splattered all over Cream. That nigga was mad as hell. I couldn't contain my laugh because he was talking plenty of shit to Puff. Puff 's ass was unbothered; he sat down and started playing the game. They called their crew to come and clean up. Once everything was good, we all went our separate ways.

25 PUFF

A FEW MONTHS LATER

"*B*ro, do you know this girl done wasted a red drink in my fucking car? So I'm headed to get my shit cleaned!" I fussed as I headed to get my car detailed. I told Nell a million times not to drive my shit. I had brought her the same damn car so that she could stay out of my shit, but she always was in mine. Today, we were going to pick her parents up from the airport, but first, I was getting my shit cleaned. I didn't want this shit to settle in my shit. I pulled up and the car wash was packed. I wasn't worried though because they were going to get on my shit before all these folks. I pulled to the stall and got out. Dre owned the car wash, so I knew that I was good. Dre and Scale ass had damn near become brothers. I was happy that Cream picked him. Dre was about his business and didn't have a problem listening.

"I'm pulling up to," Cream said before ending the call. I got out and went to find Dre's ass. That nigga was in the office getting his dick sucked. A few week back, he found out that his baby mama had cheated on him, and every since, his ass been wilding.

"Really nigga?" I laughed, closing the door back. I walked to the waiting area just as my brother was pulling up. Soon as Cream walked in, Dre came out of his office.

"You a nasty ass nigga," I said, getting up walking to his office. When we walked in, ole girl was fixing her hair. She didn't say shit before walking out. "Damn she thick," I said, watching her ass. All my ass could do was look. Nellie's ass was crazy, so there was no way that I was going to play around with her ass.

"Y'all niggas old... I'm a long rich nigga. What's else is there for me to do?" he shrugged. He wasn't lying. He was young and rich. Him and Scale was the dream team. They were bringing in so much money.

We chilled until they were done with our cars. Once mine was done, I headed home because we had an hour before it was time to pick up her parents. I pulled up at home and Nellie was in the front yard fucking with all these damn plants she had. I hated plants but my baby loved them, so it was what it was.

"Hey beautiful," I said to her as I hugged her from the back. We had been in our new house for a few months now, and she was so in love with it that she didn't won't to go anywhere. Well that and the fact that she was eight months pregnant. She swore that the baby always had her tired. She turned around and kissed me. That shit had my dick hard as always.

"*He* can lay his ass down. We have some where to be," she said, pulling away for me.

"Damn baby, it won't take long... let me put the tip in," I laughed. Nell stopped walking and just looked at me. She knew that I was addicted to her shit. My baby had the best pussy ever, hands down. I was in her shit every time I got a chance.

"Nigga, that line may have worked in 2000 but not going

to happen. I tell you what though, tonight I will let you have yo way baby," she said, kissing me. I just smiled because she knew that I was going to do the most. She grabbed her purse then we jumped in her truck. She couldn't get in my shit, period. I was going to hide all of my damn keys.

On the way to the airport, she didn't say much. I knew that she was worried if her pops would like me because I heard her talking to Peaches about it. I didn't care if they liked me or not. I was still going to make her my wife. When we pulled up, they were already standing out, which I was happy about. I hated waiting. I pulled to the curb and got out. Nellie sat there because she knew not to open the door. I was her man and that was my job. I opened the door and soon as I did, she ran straight to her parents. That shit warmed a nigga's heart. I loved seeing my baby happy.

"Mom, Dad, this is Donald, my boyfriend," she introduced us.

"Nice to meet you Donald," they both spoke. I loaded the bags in the car while her father helped them in the car. He got in the front because she wanted to get in the back with her mom. I texted the chef to see was the food ready. I knew for sure that they were hungry. We all made small talk as we headed to the house. When we pulled up, me and her dad helped the ladies out the car and we stayed back. He wanted to talk to me. I prayed that he wasn't on the bullshit because I wasn't the one.

"Son, I just wanted to say thank you for taking care of my baby and for protecting her. I don't want you to think that we didn't care. If she would have told me, I would have killed his ass years ago," her father said. We talked about a few more things then headed in the house. From talking to him, I knew that he used to be in the streets because he knew too much. I didn't want to be out here long because Cream would coming looking for my ass.

"Darrell? Nigga, is that you?" her father said soon as we walked in the door. Pops turned around, smiling.

"Monte? Nigga, what's the odds?" Pops greeted him.

"Y'all know each other daddy?" Nellie said as she walked in the room.

"You remember I used to tell you about your Uncle Dee?" he asked her.

"Yes, you said that he moved across the United States and y'all lost contact." Now, I was putting two and two together. This was Pops' friend that he always talked about. He said that he had gotten out the game years ago.

"Well, this him." They looked so happy to see each other. They walked off to the back to talk. I took a seat on the couch next to Peaches. I could see in her face that something was wrong. I got up and went to find Cream. He was outside smoking.

"Nigga, something wrong with Peaches." He passed me the blunt and rushed in the door. I put it out and walked behind him. Peaches was laid back on the couch and Nellie's mom was rubbing her head with a towel.

"It hurts Cream," she cried out. Nellie wasn't in here. I think she had went to the bathroom, but when she heard Peaches, she came running. Hell, I didn't know she could move that damn fast.

"I'm going to get the truck," Pops alerted us. They got Peaches in the car and the rest of us piled in Nellie's truck and headed to the hospital.

26 PEACHES

*J*don't think I had ever felt pain like this before. It was like the pain was constant. Hell, I didn't think that I could take it much longer. While we were in the car, I told Cream to call my mom. She had been out of rehab for a few weeks and I was so proud of her. After she OD'd, I thought that I was going to lose her, but God spared her life. I would forever be grateful for that. I just prayed that she stayed on the right track. We had purchased her a little house not too far from ours. I didn't want her in the hood because I knew that she was going to go back to her old ways.

I had been having contractions all damn day. I just hadn't said anything because I knew how important today was Nellie and I didn't want to ruin it. It seemed that as the day went on, they got worst. Now here I was getting ready to give birth to my babies. I was so ready to meet them. I had them both their own rooms and they were connected. I wanted them to have everything that I wanted as a kid. In the beginning, I wasn't happy about having twins, but then I thought about the fact that they would always have each other. Hell, I wished that my mom would have had another child. Then I wouldn't have felt alone.

"Mom, I need you to give me a big push," the doctor instructed. I looked at Cream and he gave me a head nod. I knew that meant that he had me. I took a deep breath and pushed. I few seconds later, I heard a baby cries. That warmed my heart. "Ok... one more big push." I closed my eyes and pushed. I few seconds later, there was another loud cry. I felt relieved and tired. I just wanted to sleep. The nurse walked over with my son, Donavan Jr., and all that sleepy shit went out the door. Cream pulled out his phone just as they were bring my beautiful daughter, Delilah Rose. Soon as I had them both, he snapped a picture. I heard crying and looked around to see my mother. She was standing by the door. I motioned for her to come over then asked the nurse to take our picture. Cream was on one side and she was on the other. I was so happy that she made it. They took the kids to the nursery and me to a room. I was hoping that I didn't have to stay too long. I wanted to be at home in my own bed.

"Thanks you baby," Cream said as he kissed me. Everyone started to come in after that. I was happy to see them, but I wanted to see my babies.

"You want something to eat sis?" Puff asked. I told him what I wanted then him and Nellie headed out the door. After a while, everyone left, so it was just me and Cream. He was sitting at my bedside on his phone. I couldn't help but admire how fine he was. I was blessed to have met a man like him. He made sure that I was happy not matter what the case was. If I wanted something, I got it.

"Baby, I want to redo our room and the living room. But I want to hire an interior decorator to do it. I want it like this." I said, showing him a house that I saw online. He took my phone and scrolled through the pictures and handed it back to me.

"Ok send me that," he said before looking back at his phone. I sent it to him and then started looking at cars. He had just gotten me a Benz but I wanted a Tesla. I was going to wait a while then ask for it. After they brought the kids in, Cream climbed in bed with me and we feed them. Shortly after, Puff finally came back with my damn food. I was so ready to eat. I ate and we all talked about random stuff, just enjoying each other's company. They left around midnight.

"Baby, I want to ask you something?" Cream said, pulling my attention from DJ.

"Yes, what's up?" I said without looking at him. After he didn't say anything else, I looked up to see him on one knee. My heart was damn near beating out of my chest.

"Peaches, you have given me something that no one else has. From the first day that I laid eyes on you, I knew that I wanted you to be mine. Now, I know that I want you to be mine forever. Will you marry me?" I couldn't talk, but I damn sure could nod my head. The ring was perfect.

"Yes baby! I will marry you!" I cried. This was a dream come true. He slid the ring on my finger and stood up and kissed me. I heard clapping and looked to see that our whole family was in the hallway watching.

"Bitch, let me see that ring," Nellie damn near yelled. Before she could get to me, her mom popped her upside the head, making us all laugh.

"Sorry ma... I forgot y'all was here," she laughed. I really thought they were all gone home. I was happy that they all could enjoy this moment with us. We all chilled until I got sleepy.

When I woke up the next day, the nurse was in the room but Cream and my kids were gone. That shit scared me. "Where are my kids?" I asked her.

"They are at the nursery getting there last check up so

y'all can get discharged. Your husband left to get their car seats," she advised.

"Ok, can you have them to bring them right back?" I requested. She nodded and headed to do as I asked. A few minutes later, my mom walked in the room . I took a moment to admire her. She had gained weight and was looking good.

"Hey baby, how you feeling?" She asked as she sat her purse down.

"Good ma. I was just scared when I woke up alone," I admitted. I seen so many movies and read books were people kids got taken. I would go crazy if that shit happened to me. My mother kissed me on the head and assured me that they were good. She helped me to the bathroom then helped me slip in some pants that Cream brought the other day.

"Ma, I'm really proud of you," I told her. She smile and finish helping me. This was the Janice that I knew and loved. I was so afraid that she would turn back to drugs, but she hadn't and I was so happy about that.

An hour later, I was headed home. The whole ride, Cream kept asking us were we ok. I didn't know what the driving was going to do. They were in there seats, buckled in. When we got home, Cream got the kids out then I got out. I wasn't about to leave my kids in this car even if he was coming right back out.

26 NELLIE

A FEW WEEKS LATER

"*Ma*," I yelled as I felt a warm liquid flowing down my leg. I was sitting in my office finishing up a paper that I had due. I had enrolled in school and was taking classes online. My parents had moved here last week and I was loving out. When I first asked, they wasn't with it, but after Pops talked to them, they were all for it. We had purchased them a house not far from us.

"What girl?" she said, walking in to the room. When she looked at me, she called for my father. I thought that I was ready until this pain started hitting my ass. Now I see why Peaches' ass was yelling like that. Puff was gone somewhere with Cream, so I told my mama to call him. I knew that he would meet us there so we headed to the hospital. When we got there, labor went so fast. I wasn't there two hours before my daughter graced us with her presence. Dawn Marie Latham was everything that I thought that she would be. She was the perfect combination of me and Puff. Well more him than me, but you get it.

"Can I hold my baby please?" I asked Puff for the third

time. He had been holding her since they brought her in the room. He was being selfish.

"Damn, you been had her for nine months," he fussed as he handed her to me. I couldn't do shit but laugh; this nigga had lost his damn mind. I looked at him and he looked like he was mad. I never seen that nigga act like this. I couldn't wait to tell Cream and Peaches. I wished I would have recorded this shit.

I fed my baby and changed her clothes again. Her clothes had been change at least two times today. Since they said that we both were good, we were getting discharged today. I was so happy about that.

"Baby, you want to stop and get something to eat before we go to the house?"

"Nah, ma said that she was going to come over and cook," I told him. My parents loved Puff. Hell, I was starting to think that they loved him more than they loved me. I was happy about that because they hated Clay's ass. Puff had even been going to church with my mom. Life was finally good for me.

It took us no time to get home. When we got there, I headed straight to the shower. I hated the way that hospitals made me feel. I don't care how many showers I took there, I never felt clean. Once I was done in the shower, I went to check on my baby. As always, her father was holding her. He was going to have her ass spoiled as hell.

I went to see what my mama was cooking. I was happy that I was able to move around. When Peaches first got home, her ass couldn't do shit. "Mama, you got it smelling good," I told her.

"You know I do this baby, and I made your favorite since you gave me a grandbaby," she said, pointing to the table. I walked over to see that she made me a peach cobbler. I couldn't wait to eat it. I hoped no one else had seen it because that was all me.

"Nell," Puff called out. I rushed to the living room because I thought something was wrong with my baby. When I walked in the room, he was holding a box. I looked at his ass crazy because he had scared me. Dawn was in her seat knocked out. I walked over to him and grabbed the box. I took the top off and there was another box. I rolled my eyes because I didn't like shit like this. Just give me what you gone give me. I opened the second one and there was a key. A Rose Royce key. I ran to the door to see that my baby had gotten me my dream truck. I always talked about this truck to him, but I didn't think that he would get it. I turned around and ran straight to him.

"Thanks baby," I killed his ass all over his face. If my mama wasn't in the kitchen, I would be on my knees sucking his dick. "Come to the room so that I can properly thank you," I said, walking off. When I made it to the room, I could hear him telling my mother to watch the baby. Soon as he walked in the room, I dropped to my knees. I pulled his shorts down and took his already hard dick into my mouth.

"Damn, Nell baby," he moaned out. I was deepthroating him and rubbing his balls at the same time. I knew that I couldn't give him any pussy, so I was going to suck his dick so good that it would make him feel like he was inside of me. I sucked him off till he came all in my mouth. Once I was done, he laid back on the bad and felled asleep. Making sure that he was good, I headed to check out my truck and see about my baby.

"Ma, where my daddy?" I asked after I fed my baby.

"Girl, him and Dee's ass gone to play golf. You know they ass act like they can't go a day without doing something," she joked. My dad and Pops were like brothers, so they damn near did everything together. They acted just like Puff and Cream.

"Let me find out you jealous."

"Girl please, I love the peace and quiet. I been happy his ass gone. When you get older, you will see ," she told me. My mom and dad had been together since they were sixteen and living together since they were eighteen. I'm sure he had gotten on her nerves a long time ago. We talked about things that she wanted to do to her house while she cooked. After she finished, I went to get Puff up. His ass was knocked out.

"Baby, get up... it's time to eat," I voiced. He just laid there. I said it once more. When he didn't get up, I decided to just let him rest.

PEACHES

A YEAR LATER

"*B*aby, the man with the bounce house just called, he said that he's at the gate," I passed the message on to Cream. Today was the twins first birthday. As y'all know, my ass was doing the most. I was giving them a carnival themed party. I had been planning it for the past few months.

"Ok baby. Can you finish this?" he said, handing me that case of drinks that he was putting in a cooler. I grabbed then and finished as he walked out the door. Once I was done with that, I headed to see if the kids were up. I wanted them to nap as long as they could so that they would enjoy the party. Lilah was always cranky when she didn't get enough sleep, so I wanted to make sure that she was good. DJ just went with the flow. He was more like me and she was just like her damn daddy.

"Peaches," I heard Nellie call out. Since they were still sleep, I headed to see what her loud ass wanted.

"Bitch, stop that yelling before you wake my damn kids up," I said as I came in the living room. Nellie was currently pregnant with their second daughter. They didn't waste any time getting pregnant again. Dawn was almost one and she was six month pregnant. Cream had me fucked up; my ass was on birth control. I was not having, any more kids right now; the ones I had was driving me crazy. He said that he wanted more hell so did I. I just didn't want them right now. Maybe when the twins turn three, we can try.

I was a wife, a mother, and a student. That was more than enough for me right now. I wanted to graduate college before having more kids. Plus, Cream was working so much that he was barley home. In the past year, he had opened two new commercial buildings and three apartment buildings, and now, he was opening a new hotel. His ass had more than enough on his plate.

"Let me shut up cause I don't have time for lady chucky mean ass." Nell was referring to my daughter; they ass didn't get along for shit in the world, but Lilah and Dawn where two peas in a pod. Dawn was the sweetest little baby; she was nothing like her parents. I just loved her.

"Stop playing with my niece," Puff said as he walked in the door holding Dawn. Puff didn't play about *his* babies as he would say.

"We all know that she acts just like you and Cream," Nellie shrugged and walked off. I had been telling her that she needed to stop before her baby came out acting like my baby, but she didn't want to listen. I finished getting all of the decorating together while I waited on Nellie's mom and my mom to come and cook.

My mom was doing so good, she was in church and everything. I was happy that she didn't fall back in into that black hole. She even had a boyfriend. Cream was mad when he found out. Him and Puff don't even speak to the man. He was a pastor at a church on the other side of town. They said that he wasn't good enough for her.

"Baby, everything outside is good, what else do you need help with?" Cream asked.

"Can you go and get the kids up?" he just nodded and walked off to do what I asked. Me and Cream got married a few months ago in Mexico. It was just us and the family. It was beautiful.

"Hey y'all," Scale's girlfriend spoke as they walked in the house. Scale and Dre had become like family to us. Cream and Puff had stepped down from the streets and let them take over. They sat the gift down that they had and headed to the back yard. Since people where coming, I headed to help Cream with the kids.

This was life. Everyone was happy and everything was going good. We all had worked hard to get to this point in life. I couldn't ask for more. Who would have known that I would end up married to a nigga that wasn't my type.